WRAITH
DEVIL DADDIES MC
BOOK 1

PEPPER NORTH

PHOTOGRAPHY BY
FURIOUSFOTOG

COVER MODEL
TONY BRETTMAN

Text copyright© 2025 Pepper North®
All Rights Reserved

Pepper North® is a registered trademark
All rights reserved.

NO AI TRAINING: Without in any way limiting the author's [and publisher's] exclusive rights under copyright, any use of this publication to "train" generative artificial intelligence (AI) technologies to generate text is expressly prohibited. The author reserves all rights to license uses of this work for generative AI training and development of machine learning language models.

PROLOGUE

"Where's Shadowridge?"

Steele turned around. A large biker stood on the other side of the pumps with his hands on his hips. He'd seen the custom cycle power into the gas station as he removed the cap from his tank at one of the numerous pumps. He continued to add fuel to his bike.

"Other side of the state."

"I've never seen that cut before. The Devil Daddies are the kings of this area," the stranger informed him with a scowl. "Passing through?"

Steele tamped down the voice in the back of his head that whispered a warning. "I'm here for a few months. My old lady is replacing the bank president while the regular one is on maternity leave."

"Got any more members with you?"

"No. I'm not claiming territory. Just protecting my own while I'm in town," Steele assured him.

"You should pay a visit to our president. He appreciates outsiders registering their presence."

"Understood. Where would I find him?" Steele asked, cloaking his automatic displeasure at the barely concealed demand. He kept his tone even to avoid aggravating the situation. This could go south quickly.

"Inferno. The large bar on the south side of town."

"I'll be there this afternoon," Steele stated.

"Ask for Lucien."

Steele nodded and turned back to top off his tank. The man moved away after a brief pause, but Steele sensed he was still under scrutiny. MC etiquette was a tricky thing. He'd pay the bar a visit when Ivy was safely inside the bank and after he shared his whereabouts with Kade and Storm, his MC's Enforcer and Vice President. They'd know what to do if he walked into trouble.

When his tank was topped off, Steele headed for a park he had passed on the way and pulled into a parking lot. He chose to back into a space with a good view of the road. Steele wanted to check if anyone would follow him before returning to the apartment they'd rented for a short term. Lounging back on his seat as if he didn't have a care in the world, he grabbed his phone and made a call.

"Hey, it's Steele. Let me talk to Kade." The MC's Enforcer would be the first person he contacted.

"Steele. Tired of that Podunk town and ready to come home?" Kade joked as he got on the line.

"Not quite yet. Ivy's enjoying the new challenge but missing her friends."

"Those Little girls love to get together."

Steele couldn't help overhearing the loud whisper in the background.

"Ask him if we can phone Ivy tonight, Daddy!"

Steele had no trouble recognizing Remi's voice.

Kade shared, "They wanted to call her last night, but I was concerned about interfering with Ivy's bedtime. I figured she was coming home exhausted after working in the new branch."

"I put her to bed at seven, and she didn't protest."

"That's telling," Kade pointed out.

AUTHOR'S NOTE:

The following story is completely fictional. The characters are all over the age of 18 and as adults choose to live their lives in an age play environment.

This is a series of books that can be read in any order. You may, however, choose to read them sequentially to enjoy the characters best. Subsequent books will feature characters that appear in previous novels as well as new faces.

You can contact me on
my Pepper North Facebook pages,
at www.4peppernorth.club
eMail at 4peppernorth@gmail.com
I'm experimenting with Instagram, Twitter, and Tiktok.
Come join me everywhere!

"Exactly. She slept well and was energized to go. How about if we call at six this evening? Think the others would be up for it?" Steele asked, anticipating that the Littles would jump on that suggestion.

"Let me tell Remi. She'll spread the word." Kade relayed the message to his Little. "Ivy will phone today at six."

"Yesssss!"

Steele could only imagine how fast Remi got on her phone to text the news. "Hey, I need to let you know I ran into a member of a local club here in town. Can you get me any information on the Devil Daddies? I'm visiting their headquarters in a bar named Inferno this afternoon."

"Are you expecting trouble? Want to delay a couple of hours? I can be there in six," Kade asked. His voice instantly hardened.

"I'm under scrutiny. Three bikes have cruised past while we've been talking. I'm either on their normal path or they're keeping me in view. It's better I go in alone. If I show up with my Enforcer, they might not be too receptive."

"Call me by four to tell me how it went," Kade demanded.

"Make it by five. That's when I'll need to pick up Ivy," Steele suggested to give himself some wiggle room. Kade would act immediately to organize an official response if he suspected something had happened to the Shadowridge Guardians' MC President.

"Got it. Be alert. Send an SOS if you need it."

Steele occupied himself in town for the rest of the morning. He had lunch out and ran some errands. He wouldn't lead the members of the Devil Daddies MC back to their apartment until he was sure Ivy would be safe. At two o'clock, he headed for Inferno.

It was definitely distinctive. A rough-hewn exterior gave the bar a weathered look. Red neon flames decorated the name along with the logo that Steele had noted on the cuts of the men who'd kept him in their sights. As he approached the immense building, Steele could see several equally large warehouses ranging behind the bar. The MC didn't operate a repair or customizing shop. Why would they need large warehouses? What were they storing? Or moving?

When he pulled into the parking lot, the crowd was already rocking. An array of bikes was backed into spaces across the front curb. Steele bypassed those to leave his bike in a less desirable space on the side. No need to ruffle feathers before he even got inside Inferno.

"Nice bike," the powerful man stationed at the door said as a greeting. He didn't stand but stayed seated on his stool. "Shadowridge Guardians."

"Yes. I'm looking for Lucien." Steele didn't introduce himself to the MC member. He needed to talk to the President first.

"He's behind the bar."

"Thanks." Steele headed inside, scanning the room to absorb the vibe. It was larger than the Hangout. He suspected it drew more of a rough crowd than the array of everyone from college-age kids to sixtysomethings who filled his hometown spot. He liked the atmosphere of Inferno. He could see what drew people here. The owner had his finger on the pulse of his clientele.

He checked out the two guys behind the bar and took his best guess. Steele headed for the heavily tattooed biker with the sides of his skull shaved and sat down on the stool in front of him. "Lucien?"

"Yeah. Who's asking?" The man's piercing green eyes didn't seem to miss much.

"I'm Steele. I ran into one of your club members at the gas station today," Steele said, keeping his tone even. There was something about this guy that screamed danger. He needed to navigate the conversation with care.

"You're on my turf," Lucien said bluntly.

"My apologies. I didn't know this town had an established

club. My old lady is here to work at a bank for a few weeks. I always travel with her."

"The Shadowridge Guardians, right?" Lucien asked.

Steele nodded. "I'm the President." It was best he got that out of the way early in their conversation.

"Yeah. You guys have a bike shop."

"I'm a welder. I specialize in custom jobs. There are a lot of great bikes out front." Steele kept his eyes on Lucien. He couldn't pick up any vibes to judge how this was going.

"Is your club coming to town?" Lucien asked.

"There are no plans for that at the present." Steele left that open. The club would be there in a flash if something happened to him.

"I understand. Keep your nose out of our business and don't try to stay permanently," Lucien warned.

"What is your business?" Steele looked pointedly at Lucien. He wasn't going to pussyfoot around.

Lucien laughed.

Steele understood the message. A giggle caught his attention. Automatically glancing toward the sound, he spotted a woman dressed in holey jeans with a pink ruffled top on the other side of the bar. Her hair was in two braids with pink ribbons.

The other man behind the bar moved to stand next to Lucien, blocking his view. That confirmed for Steele that Devil Daddies wasn't just a name. He didn't address the man who'd joined them but directly met Lucien's gaze.

"The Shadowridge Guardians protect those with tender hearts and feelings. They're off-limits."

Lucien studied him for a long moment before reaching across the bar to offer his hand. "I'll hold you to that."

"Likewise," Steele declared before shaking the man's hand. While this was promising, he would remain on guard while they were in town.

His business done, Steele stood. Feeling the prickle of at least a dozen eyes on his back, Steele walked confidently to the front door. The guard at the entrance had disappeared. They wouldn't touch him now.

He reached his bike and sent Kade a message:

We have some Little things in common with the Devil Daddies. There will be no problems here.

The response came instantly, confirming for Steele that Kade had prepared to ride if he'd sent a different message.

Got it. Devil Daddies. Don't start wearing horns.

Not going to happen. I'll stick with my Guardian wings.

Steele fired up his bike and drove from the parking lot. He'd accomplished his mission. His Little girl would be safe here in town.

CHAPTER 1

A week after Lucien updated the MC about a Shadowridge Guardian's presence in town, no other bikers had arrived from that MC. While that eased their concern, the Devil Daddies continued to be vigilante for a takeover, but it appeared that Steele's word was good. He did not plan to challenge them for territory. Lucien's focus returned to Inferno and the warehouses. He did place his Enforcer at the door, just in case there was trouble.

Wraith stretched his back. He hadn't done door duty for a long time. Sitting just inside the door, he screened each person who wished to enter. Maintaining that level of evaluation demanded focus. He'd need to rotate guys there more often. One wrong decision could be problematic.

"Go home. This isn't a good place for you," he growled at a woman wearing a knee-length full skirt and a cardigan. Really? A cardigan? At a biker bar?

"But I need to see…."

"Not going to happen. Head back to your car." Wraith slid off his stool and stood to tower over the Sunday school or kindergarten teacher. As he expected, she spun and raced toward the parking lot. She had to be the same one who'd tried to come in last night.

Shaking his head, Wraith checked out the next person in line. His gaze met deep brown eyes that skittered away from his. Instantly, he was on alert. That reaction usually signaled a fake ID. He scanned her curvy body, guesstimating her weight and height to compare with the ID she presented.

"Eyes on me," he barked.

This time, she looked at him directly. Her gorgeous appearance sent shockwaves straight to his dick. Those eyes dominated a heart-shaped face. And those red lips? He wondered what she'd taste like. Clamping down on his control, Wraith held his hand out.

Caroline Sweets, 32, address in the upper east side, height 5'7", weight 194.

He was impressed. Not many states still required it—probably because most people lied, Wraith guessed. She'd told the license bureau her real weight. That almost never happened. Caroline matched her picture perfectly. This wasn't a fake ID.

"Welcome, Caroline. Have fun," he said as he handed back the small card. He turned to watch her walk past. *Damn, that ass was biteable.*

"Can I enter?"

A fake, high voice brought his attention back to the next person in line who fluttered her artificial lashes at him. "Betty. You're always welcome. Have fun!" he greeted one of their regulars, who'd come in to flirt with his biker buddies.

Wraith scanned the room, checking the space for crowding. The Devil Daddies never allowed enough people in to fill the room to total capacity. A rough crowd packed in like sardines led to a lot of exploding tempers. Add alcohol and the place was a tinderbox.

His gaze skirted over Caroline. Standing in the shadows, she'd tucked herself into a corner, typing frantically on her phone as she tried to look everywhere at the same time. What was she up to? When her roving scan met his, Caroline shifted slightly to the left behind a couple standing by a table.

Instantly, his problem radar went into overdrive. Making a mental note to keep an eye on her, Wraith turned back to those in line. "Tom! You're not allowed in for two more weeks. Get out of here."

"Come on, Wraith. I'll be super quiet. You won't even know I'm inside," Tom assured him. The bruises scattered over his face had reached the point of turning green from the ugly fight.

"Nope. Lucien decreed you're banned until next month. I'm not going to tell him I'm countermanding his decision. I like my pretty face without bruises."

"You're not his pussy, are you?" the belligerent man asked and let out a yelp as a biker in a Devil Daddies cut yanked him backward out of the doorway.

"I'll teach this one a lesson, Wraith," Scythe called as he dragged the man from the entrance.

"Hey! Wait! I'll leave," Tom assured him. His voice faded as Scythe towed him away from the building.

Wraith looked back to the next man in line. He'd buy Scythe a drink the next time they were at the bar together. Wraith owed him one for handling that hothead. Tom obviously needed to be barred another month from Inferno.

Throughout the evening, Wraith spotted Caroline in various locations in the bar. Sticking to herself, she often cradled a glass of red wine in one hand and her phone in the other. She fascinated him for reasons he didn't fully understand. Caroline's beauty drew him, but her actions intrigued him. What was she doing here?

When he saw Hellcat heading her way, Wraith called Scythe to take over. Without asking a question, Scythe slid into place and started checking IDs.

Wraith merged into the crowd. He checked the spot where he'd last seen her, but it was empty. He walked toward the stairs leading up to the office space to look over everyone's head. *There she is!* Wraith set off on a path to intercept her.

"What are you doing, Caroline?" he barked over the music.

When she jumped several inches from the ground in fright, Wraith almost felt bad. "How do you know my name?" she gasped after whirling to face him.

"ID, remember?"

"You can't remember everyone's name," she protested.

"I can. Now, back to my question. Why are you slinking around? Are you casing people?"

"What? No!" Caroline seemed to realize she was attracting attention. She leaned closer to speak softer. "I'm not a criminal! I'm a… people watcher. I love to observe everyone in different situations."

"A people watcher. So, a stalker," Wraith suggested, backing her up until her body touched the wall. He braced one hand against the worn wood paneling, trapping her in place.

"I am not a stalker," she hissed at him. "Oh, shit!"

Before Wraith could ask any more questions, she wrapped a hand around the back of his head and pulled his lips to hers. It took a lot to distract Wraith from his objective. Her kiss far exceeded that threshold.

Wraith tangled his fingers in the silky tresses that cascaded down her back and pulled. When she moaned with excitement at the faint touch of pain, he deepened the kiss. Her arousing taste hinted at the red wine she'd sipped. Somehow, it bewitched him. He leaned forward to pin her to the wall, loving the feel of her soft curves pressed against him.

He explored her mouth slowly, savoring her. She grabbed a handful of his T-shirt and held him close as she met each of his kisses fully. His shaft throbbed against the fly of his jeans, instantly alert.

"Get a room, Wraith."

The amused voice reminded him of where they were. He didn't even check to see who had spoken to him when he didn't recognize the voice. He didn't matter. She did. Wraith pressed one last gentle kiss to her lips before lifting his head to stare into her brown eyes.

"We need to get out of here," he growled. He wouldn't fuck her in some cubbyhole in the back room. Wraith needed to take his time with this delicious treat.

"Sorry. My ex just walked by. He's not a nice person. The only way I could think of hiding from him was to kiss you. Then…."

Wraith didn't let her off the hook. He needed to hear how she finished that statement.

"Then… I've never felt anything like that." Her enormous eyes searched his face.

"I'm sorry you've been with crappy lovers, Temptress. All your kisses should be that striking."

"I think it's you," she whispered.

"Do you want to leave?" he asked.

"You mean go somewhere else and…."

"Yeah. Better than here in the hallway. I don't share."

"I don't… I don't do that."

"Fuck?" he asked and loved the fierce blush that spread over her face and chest. She couldn't be more desirable. Well, at least not clothed. Caroline was a present he couldn't wait to unwrap.

"Could you get more crass?" she asked, bristling.

"Yes. That's not a problem. My crass level is epic," he teased her. The stiffness seeped out of her tense form. Her eyes focused back on his mouth, making his heavy shaft twitch inside his now-tight jeans. "You're killing me, Temptress. What do you say? Shall we get out of here?"

"We have to go to my place," she announced, obviously needing to seize control.

Wraith would allow her to do that. Later when they were alone, she'd discover who was always going to be in charge. "Okay. I'll ride with you."

"Don't you have a bike or something?"

"I do. But I'm not letting you out of my sight. I can Uber back or call a Devil Daddy to come get me."

"Do you do this often?"

"Never." He let that reassurance hang in the air.

"Really?"

"I'm picky when it comes to choosing a partner, Caroline. I have a feeling you are too. You'll be safe. I got tested months ago when my last relationship ended."

"You'll have to wear a condom," she declared, as if searching for something that would take this decision out of her hands.

"No problem. I'm a grown-ass man."

Wraith watched her face, picking up her progression of thoughts. He saw she'd run out of demands and hadn't found anything to convince herself he was off limits. He cupped her face and lowered his lips to hers once again and kissed her until they were both breathing heavily. He didn't need proof that this attraction between them was explosive, but she did. Wraith recognized how rare it was to experience this level of sexual excitement.

"Ready to leave?"

When she nodded, he wrapped an arm around her waist and guided her toward the back entrance. At the door, he told Fury, the biker manning that access point, "I'm out of here. Don't call me."

"Got it, Wraith." Fury didn't even look at the woman he escorted out. Wraith's business was his.

The corner of Wraith's mouth quirked up on one side. If he had his way, the club would understand Caroline was under his protection soon. She might be planning a one-night stand, but he wasn't.

CHAPTER 2

Caroline's mind raced. She couldn't believe she was letting this biker pick her up. She stole a sideways glance at his handsome face and hard body. Caroline's practical side told her to go for it. No man ever looked at her like this guy did.

"I don't even know your name," she whispered, appalled as she stopped in her tracks.

"Wraith."

"Oh." They walked through the parking lot.

"Do you remember where you left your car?"

"There was a huge boulder at the end of the row," Caroline shared.

"Got it. Come on."

They walked past a row of cars and bikes until Caroline stopped in her tracks. A shadowy figure sat on her back bumper a short distance away. "That's Adam. He found my car."

"Shall we go on my bike, or should I take care of him?" Wraith asked.

Take care of him? What did that mean? Caroline pushed the question of how the burly biker would deal with her ex out of her mind. Then she squashed the flare of interest that ignited inside her at the thought of someone intimidating Adam. She'd love to see the tables turned on her ex for once.

"Your bike. I don't want him to hurt my car."

"On it." Wraith directed their path to the side of the building. Caroline had noticed a lot of bikes sporting the Devil Daddies logo there when she'd walked in. What was he going to say when he found out she'd never ridden a bike?

Wraith pulled out his phone and placed a call. "Hey, Wraith here. I'm out for the night. There's an asshole hanging next to a woman's car in the parking lot. Row eight, east side." He hung up without saying anything else.

"What will they do to him?"

"He'll get tossed out."

"Adam won't like that," Caroline warned.

"I can live with that. Can you?" he asked, never stopping.

She didn't bother to answer. The moment Adam asked her for a divorce after four and a half years of marriage was the end of her concern for him. She bumped into Wraith's powerful body on purpose, enjoying the contact with his hard form.

Caroline cocked her head to the side to look up at his handsome face surreptitiously. She'd never done anything like this before. If she had to break every rule she'd followed in her sparse dating activities before Adam, having a one-night fling with Wraith would be worth it.

Besides, she could use the experience of hot sex with a stranger in her book. Her love life hadn't inspired a lot of sexy scenes. Or, it hadn't until now.

"Ready?"

"Yes."

"Good girl."

A thrill filled her. She couldn't believe how those two words could resonate inside her. Of course, he didn't mean that phrase the way she took it. Caroline's eyes landed on the club patch on his cut. Devil Daddies.

"Are you a Daddy?" she blurted before she could stop herself.

"Yes."

Wraith didn't stop walking toward the bikes. He did squeeze her hand. There was no way he meant that in the same way she did. Or did he? Hope flared inside her.

Caroline tried to figure out what to say. Maybe he had children, and they were talking about different things.

"How many kids do you have?" she asked, testing the waters.

"No offspring. No adult Little girl either. Here's my bike."

"Oh," she said, unsure of how to respond to that. She'd asked, and he'd answered. Her pulse quickened. He was a Daddy Dom.

He stopped at an old-school chopper with ape-hanger handlebars. Caroline had learned those terms from her internet searches about bikes and riders. A zing of pride flowed through her. She'd put a lot of dedication into this new series. It appeared everything was soaking in.

All those thoughts dissolved when Wraith leaned over to unfasten the buckles on his leather saddlebags. He had obviously not skipped leg and butt day. Caroline had never been with anyone so built.

When he turned around, she found herself staring at his fly. *Holy crap!* He cleared his throat, and her gaze flew up to meet his.

'Sorry. I….'" What did she say to excuse staring at his erection?

"I like the package you come in too, Little girl. Let's get this helmet on you so we can go explore."

While she squeezed her thighs together in reaction to the arousal that flooded her at being called that, he stepped forward to brush her hair over her shoulders and gathered it into a thick ponytail. Before she realized what he was doing, Wraith tucked her tresses into the back of her shirt. "You'll get less tangled this way."

With that accomplished, he grabbed the helmet he'd pulled out of his saddlebag from the seat and fit it over her head. In a few quick moves, he fastened the chinstrap.

As he put on his own, Wraith told her, "I'll get on first and start the bike. When I have it stabilized, you'll step over and sit up here." He patted a slightly higher section of the seat that had a metal loop as a backrest.

"Okay." She was relieved she didn't have to admit she was clueless.

Stepping back as he swung a leg over the wide bike, Caroline watched him start the engine and then brace the machine between his thick thighs.

"Come on, Temptress."

Awkwardly, she tried to straddle the bike with as much ease as he had. Her heel caught on the metal bar, and she wobbled on one foot. Without saying a word, Wraith wrapped an arm around her, stabilizing her and helping her settle on the seat.

"Put your feet up on the pegs and hold on to me," he instructed when she'd settled into place with a sigh of relief.

It took a few seconds for her to find the footrests. As she squirmed around, panicking that she was so uncool, Wraith's large hand wrapped around her thigh. He guided her leg to the right place, easily controlling her jerky movements without any apparent judgement.

"You've got this," he assured her calmly.

"Thanks," she whispered and relaxed.

His hands pulled hers in front of him, tugging her arms around his powerful torso. "Hold on, Caroline. Lean the way I do, even if it seems scary. I've got you. I'll keep you safe."

Adam shouted from across the parking lot where Caroline's car sat. "You can't kick me out for waiting for my wife. Call the police. I'm not leaving."

Wraith kicked the stand up into place and eased the bike out of his spot. Dismissing her concern about her ex, she decided she'd missed too much already while married to him. Caroline hugged herself to him, burying her nose in his back. She inhaled Wraith's masculine scent as they crept through the parking lot. Stiffening her resolve, Caroline didn't glance toward the growing commotion on the other side of the lot. Adam was on his own.

Riding with Wraith was both terrifying and exhilarating. Corners were the scariest. If she'd been able to unlock her hands from where they were frozen around Wraith's waist, Caroline was sure she could have touched the pavement whizzing by a scant foot away. She definitely couldn't concentrate on anything else as they sped through town.

On a long, straight stretch, Caroline relaxed a bit. The roar of the motor between her legs built heat inside her—both sexy arousal and actual warmth. She understood what all the MC romance books meant by the throbbing engine against her most private space. Caroline didn't know what was more arousing, holding on to Wraith's hard body or feeling the vibrations.

She shifted her hands slightly and froze. Caroline couldn't mistake what she'd touched. Without thinking, she stroked her fingers over the thick shaft. A powerful hand clamped over hers.

"You're going to make me drop the bike, Temptress," he yelled back to her.

She'd never be able to look at him again. Caroline tried to draw her hands back to hold on to his waist, and Wraith tugged her into position again.

"You don't want me to pull this bike over."

The implied threat in there didn't scare her. His stern tone sent an extra thrill through her. Caroline tried to relax, but the new sensations, scents, and views excited her. She could love riding on a bike if she got to hang on to Wraith.

"One-night stand, remember," she told herself firmly.

A thought popped into her head. Why hadn't she said something earlier? "Do you need directions?"

"What?" he shouted back to her over the motor.

"Directions?"

"I've got it," he assured her and turned off the main road.

How much had he memorized from her driver's license? Oh, my God! He knew her weight. That panicked thought reverberated in her head for a few more turns. *He doesn't care. He'd had her private information from the beginning.*

She relaxed against him once again. He lifted one hand from the handlebars to wrap it around her leg, squeezing it slightly. Wraith caressed the length of her thigh. She noted that his were larger than hers. That shouldn't make a difference, she told herself, but it did. Caroline liked big, burly guys. Unfortunately, they all seemed to go for the petite cheerleader type.

She crossed her fingers, hoping to have one magical night with the drop-dead gorgeous man. It was her turn to get the guy. Even if it was for a short time. Caroline had realized looking back she should have listened to that voice in the back of her mind. She was definitely going to heed its encouragement now.

He turned into the condos where she now rented. Getting away from her previous house was the best thing that could have happened. It didn't hold good memories for her.

"I'm in the third one on the left. You can park in the garage if you'd like," she told him.

He turned into the driveway and steadied the bike so she could dismount and enter the garage door code. Wraith also caught her when she got off-kilter. He didn't make a big deal of it but wrapped his arms around her until she had her vibrating legs back under control.

"Thanks," she whispered, staring into his dark eyes.

"Go open the door. I don't want an audience when I make you come," he told her, patting her full bottom.

"Oh!" What could she say to that? The combination of his blunt words and intimate touch did funny things to her inside. Caroline dashed to the controls and keyed in her code. The garage door didn't move. Panicking, she tried it one more time. Still nothing. Crap! Wanting to whack herself on the forehead, she remembered to push the star that activated the connection. Slowly, the door inched upward.

Following him inside, she waited for him to make a big deal about her screwup. To her surprise, he simply drew her close to unfasten and remove her helmet. He stripped off his as well and set both on the seat of his motorcycle.

"Invite me in, Caroline."

She stepped forward to press a quick kiss on his lips before shifting back to take his hand. Tugging him to the door, she said, "Follow me." Thank goodness Wraith remembered to press the button lowering the door.

Once inside, he asked, "Bedroom? Living room? Kitchen table?"

CHAPTER 3

"Kitchen table?" she repeated, struggling to keep her jaw from dropping.

"We'll save that for round two."

"We will?"

He didn't answer but scooped her up in his arms. Instantly, Caroline froze, afraid to off-balance him. Surely, he couldn't handle her weight. "Where's your bedroom, Little girl?"

"Upstairs. I can walk. I'm too heavy," she blurted. How embarrassing would it be for him to have a heart attack halfway up the steps?

Wraith shifted her effortlessly, lifting her up to drape over his shoulder. "No comfy ride for a Little who speaks badly about herself." He smacked her bottom with a ringing slap and turned to stalk up the stairs.

Afraid to move in case she pushed him off-balance, Caroline stayed as still as possible. *Little? Oh, God. He is a Daddy!* That slight taste of punishment made her wonder what a real spanking would feel like. Her gaze focused on his rounded ass. The powerful muscles flexed with each step he climbed. His heart rate didn't seem to change at all.

When he reached the top of the stairs, he stalked into the

bedroom at the end of the hall, guessing correctly that it was hers. With a flick, he turned on the overhead fixture. Bright light flooded the room. He popped off her sandals as he strode forward to the bed and tossed them into the corner before setting her feet on the carpet.

"Sorry?" she squeaked.

"You'll learn," he answered cryptically before stalking over to the blinds and closing them tightly. He returned to her side and sat on the edge of the bed before drawing her between his legs. "This wasn't safe, Little girl. Picking up a man in a biker bar."

"Are you going to hurt me?" she asked, surprised that she wasn't afraid of him at all. Pure excitement and anticipation filled her.

"I'm going to spank your butt for taking such a chance and then I'm going to make you come so many times you'll wonder which one was the punishment," Wraith told her as he reached for the button at the top of her jeans.

He had it unfastened and the zipper pulled down before she had processed that statement. "That's a big promise," she said with a laugh, trying to be cool, while mentally praying he wouldn't be disappointed in her body.

"Fact, Temptress."

He hooked his fingers into her waistband and pulled the heavy denim down to her knees before she could react. In another split second, he'd draped Caroline over his hard thighs. His hand rubbed over the red lace panties she'd worn to feel daring.

"These are pretty. I'd love to see you in flowery cotton or perhaps something padded."

Caroline's brain went into overload at that statement. Cotton like Little girl panties? Padded? He didn't mean diapers, did he? Did Daddies really like those? Surely that only happened in books.

He hooked a finger into the waistband of the frilly garment and slowly dragged them over her skin. She had plenty of time to protest but had no intention of missing a spanking from this man. How could he sense that was one of her fantasies?

With her panties dragged to her knees as well, he stroked his hand over her naked flesh. His touch felt electric. Caroline was so wet. She glanced over her shoulder, afraid that her curves would have turned him off. The ravenous hunger on his face erased that worry from her mind.

His hand rose and hesitated. That brief pause caused her anticipation to mingle with sudden doubts. What was she doing? Caroline bit her lip to keep herself from begging him to let her go. She wasn't going to allow herself to wimp out now. His palm descended quickly. Warmth flared over her skin.

"Ouch!" she yelped.

"You didn't think your spanking would hurt?" he asked, adding two more sharp swats.

"No!" she blurted, lying. Reality stung much harder than it sounded in a sexy book.

"Tonight's a perfect time to learn."

Wraith scattered each slap in a different spot on her bottom and upper thighs. Each spank left a patch of warmth that seared into her brain. Caroline sagged over his lap as the heat grew. Soon, the burn blended together.

"You are taking your spanking so well, Little girl. You are not to put yourself at risk. Do you promise me?"

"But...." How could he lecture her on picking up men when he was the one she'd chosen?

"You are too precious to risk yourself like this."

"Precious?" she echoed.

His next spank landed on the seam of her pussy. Caroline gasped as the fire on her skin seemed to ignite inside her as well. She squirmed on his lap, not wanting to get away but needing more. When he repeated his target, a moan tumbled from her lips, and her hands closed around his thick calf, needing to touch him.

"Naughty girls who take their spankings well earn rewards, Caroline. Do you think you deserve one?" Wraith asked.

Without hesitating, she nodded. She couldn't get the words to form in her mind as she split her attention between her punishment and the growing arousal inside her. Never had she wanted to come this much.

"Spread your legs," he ordered in a low, husky voice that told her he was turned on as well.

Eagerly, Caroline inched her thighs apart as far as possible with the jeans and panties bunched around her knees. She inhaled sharply when instead of a swat, Wraith drew two fingers through the wetness between her legs. He traced her cleft, igniting so many sensitive spots.

He inhaled deeply. A second later he said, "I can smell your sweet juices, Temptress. Can I taste you safely?"

She had to repeat that in her mind to digest that question. He didn't rush her or repeat himself. Wraith simply waited for her answer.

"I got tested after my divorce. I didn't trust him. Everything came back okay."

"I'm glad you took care of yourself. Let me see if you taste as sweet as your scent."

Caroline peeked over her shoulder. Wraith lifted his fingers to his mouth and sucked them inside. She'd never seen anything so erotic. Forget the pornos she'd tried to watch for research. Wraith was sex incarnate.

"Mmm." His low voice drew the sound out several syllables. The rumble sent a shiver down her spine. "I'm going to enjoy you, Little girl."

"How do you know?" she asked. How could he be so sure she was Little?

Wraith stroked his fingers through her wetness again. This time, he explored her pink folds, caressing her. Her eyes wavered on the edge of crossing when he answered, "Daddy radar. Do you want to tell me I'm wrong?"

After hesitating for a few seconds to decide how honest she should be, Caroline answered him. "You're not wrong. You're also the first person I've ever admitted that to."

"Lying to me is a bad idea. Telling me the truth is smart."

Wraith stood, lifted and rotated Caroline, and set her on the bed. She hissed as her hot bottom touched the comforter. She'd feel that for a day, at least. Distracted by those thoughts, she missed Wraith stripping her jeans and panties completely off.

His gaze roamed over her. Feeling self-conscious, Caroline covered her mound. How long had it been since she'd trimmed down there?

"Never hide from me."

Slowly, she inched her hands away and pressed them flat to the covers. *Please don't be mean.* Caroline closed her eyes to shut out what she was sure would be a negative reaction. Adam had always had something negative to say—a suggestion they throw out the cookies she'd baked for him, a mention of a coupon in the paper for a discounted waxing at the salon, or some equally demeaning comment.

His moan made her peek back at him. The hunger written on his face eased her nervousness. When his movement caught her attention, it evaporated. She bit her lip as he stroked a rough hand over the fly of his jeans. The thick shaft penned inside jerked in reaction.

Wraith lowered himself to his knees in front of her. He wrapped his hand around her ankle and tugged her forward until her hot butt dangled partially off the mattress.

"Spread your legs, Precious."

She inched her thighs apart.

"More, Caroline. I need to see your pretty kitty."

Those growled words sent a shiver down her spine as she followed his directions.

"More."

When she stopped again, Caroline knew he could see how wet she was. Losing her nerve, she opened her mouth to tell him this was a bad idea but snapped it shut as he reached over his head to drag his T-shirt off and toss it away.

Needing a better view, she propped herself up on an elbow. He'd looked built with clothes on. Now she wanted to trace the deep grooves in his muscles with her tongue.

Where did that come from? Astonished by her reactions to him, Caroline quickly abandoned an effort to figure out why. This hot biker made her desire to be wild.

Wraith shifted forward between her legs. When she automatically tried to pull her thighs together, he clamped his hands over her knees, stopping that motion. "No hiding, Caroline. Not tonight."

She nodded before she realized what she was doing. Was he mesmerizing her? Why did she want to do exactly what he said?

"Good girl."

His praise fueled the fire inside her. Caroline hoped to please him more than anything she'd ever craved before. She bit her lip as her body responded with a gush of slickness.

Wraith leaned forward, lowering his head toward her pussy. He inhaled deeply and smiled. *That's a wolfish grin!* Caroline was so using that in a book.

He pressed a kiss to the top of her cleft. His beard scratched against her sensitive skin. She loved the sensation and yearned for more. Would he?

Wraith flicked his tongue out to taste her. This time, his approving hum vibrated through her. She held her breath as he moved. He lashed his tongue across her pussy, teasing her as he shifted lower. His beard and mustache prickled her skin, making it feel like a thousand tiny barbs stroking her.

She lifted her hips, pressing herself toward the teasing touch of his mouth. Wraith rewarded her by exploring her pink folds. He traced her inner lips and dipped his tongue into her pussy. Caroline gasped as his mustache brushed over her clit. When he repeated the action and slid two thick fingers into her, Caroline grabbed handfuls of the comforter below her. His calloused skin rubbed over sensitive spots she'd never known existed. The combination of all those sensations pushed her to the brink.

"Come, Little girl," he growled against her.

The order pushed her over the edge. A climax erupted inside her, shaking her with its strength. Wraith returned to his intimate kisses, stretching and building the pleasure until she thought she'd black out.

Releasing her death-grip on the bedding, Caroline raised a hand and curled it around the back of his head. "Enough. I can't take anymore."

Wraith lifted his mouth away from her to run his gaze over her before meeting Caroline's. "We're a long way from finished, Precious. That was simply round one." He pressed a last kiss to her mound as he slid his fingers from her.

Caroline abandoned her attempt to pull herself together when he sucked his fingers clean. "You're in charge," she whispered.

"I've always been in charge, Little girl. I'm glad you understand that now."

CHAPTER 4

Wraith crawled onto the bed, prowling over her. He couldn't resist the temptation of the half-dressed woman in front of him. Caging her underneath him, Wraith kissed her hard, sharing the flavor of her essence that still coated his lips and mustache. To his delight, she responded and licked his skin when the fiery kiss ended. She was a sensual creature to the core.

"Let's get the rest of your clothes off, Caroline."

When she wiggled underneath him to grab the bottom of her shirt, he shook his head at her. "I get to unwrap my present."

"Oh."

Her instant submission made his cock jerk in his jeans. She was absolutely perfect. How had anyone ever let her get away?

Wraith pushed himself up to sit, allowing a small portion of his weight to rest on her pelvis. He tugged her hands from the hem of her top and pulled the garment over her head. She cooperated beautifully, raising her arms so he could get rid of it.

"Damn, you're beautiful, Caroline." Wraith took a quick second to memorize the sight of her in a matching red lace bra. He ran a finger under a shoulder strap.

"Were you planning on picking someone up?" he asked, lifting an eyebrow quizzically.

"No!" She shook her head emphatically, as if the suggestion horrified her.

"Okay, sweetheart. I already knew I was a lucky man. Some things can't be denied." He followed the strap over the shape of her full breasts and loved her quick inhale of breath. "We need to get this off you now."

With a few practiced moves, he unfastened the clasp behind her and eased the lace forward. He could feel her gaze glued to his face and allowed her to see his appreciation of her curves as he tossed that garment onto the growing pile.

"So pretty." Wraith cupped her breasts, gently rolling the soft flesh in his hands.

"I wonder if you taste as delicious as you look?" He leaned down to press his mouth to the sensitive side of her breast and trailed kisses to one deep-red nipple. Taking the taut peak into his mouth, he repeated the brushing motion of his tongue that had worked so well for her much lower. Her moan assured him she loved the whisking sensation here as well.

"Wraith. I want to see you too. Take these off," she demanded, wrapping her hands around his thighs.

He loved this side of her. Before he moved, Wraith nipped at the nipple trapped in his mouth to remind her who was in charge. He released his target with an audible pop before pressing his hands to the mattress.

Reversing his path, Wraith pushed himself up to standing and popped the button open on his now too-tight jeans. Wraith was more aroused than he could remember. He thrust a hand into the front to cup himself and drew the zipper down to avoid injury to his steel-hard erection. Nicking his cock with those metal teeth was not in his plans tonight.

Caroline stared so hard at his crotch he could almost feel her touching him. Controlling his grin at her eagerness, Wraith wrapped his hand around the base of his erection and tugged his hand toward the tip. He wasn't twelve inches of porn star endowed, but he'd never had complaints. As her eyes widened, he knew negative comments wouldn't start now.

"That's never going to fit," she whispered.

"We're going to be just fine, Little girl."

She shook her head in disbelief. "I don't think I can even get my mouth around that," she protested.

That visual image made his cock jump. "Maybe we'll try later." He quickly removed the rest of his clothing. He grabbed a condom from his pocket and rejoined her on the bed.

Wraith wrapped his arms around her and boosted her up to the pillow before kissing a path back to her mouth. Her hands closed around his shoulders. He could tell she was nervous. That was fine. He had all the time in the world.

Seducing her with long, steamy kisses, Wraith stroked his hands over her rounded curves. He'd never understood the allure of hard, bony women. His preference had always been those whose softness contrasted with his muscular form.

When her hands relaxed their grip and roamed over him, Wraith pressed a thigh between her legs, offering her something to squirm against. The feel of her wetness grinding on his quad told him she was ready. He quickly rolled the condom into place before moving fully over her.

Wraith dragged one of her legs up around his waist and pressed the head of his cock to her opening. Feeling her wetness directly on his skin would be incredible. Inside, he shook that away. He'd used protection since he was fifteen. Never had he regretted the thin sheath around him.

Her fingers dug into his sides, signaling she had gotten nervous again. Wraith shifted slightly and slid his shaft through her pink folds, targeting her clit. He wasn't in any hurry. If she needed time, he had hours to help her be ready.

"I've got you, Little girl. I'm never going to hurt you," he assured her before capturing her mouth in a sizzling kiss.

She melted into his arms. He loved how responsive she was. Caressing her breasts and down her abdomen, Wraith searched for her most responsive spots and teased those. Brushing his thumb over her clit as he glided his erection through her wetness, he could feel her tense and then, a moment later, combust.

Her nails dug into his shoulders as Caroline enjoyed the climax that shook her body. He'd have marks as a souvenir to treasure.

Two.

Driving her wild had become his favorite pastime.

Shifting slightly, Wraith pressed the head of his cock into her. Her muscles quivered around him as he glided into her heat. Her snug passage made him groan with delight. Being inside Caroline had become his favorite place on earth.

"You feel like heaven," he told her as he slowly filled her.

"Don't stop. Please," she begged.

"Never," Wraith promised her.

When he slid the last inch into place, Wraith dropped his forehead down to hers and paused to control his urge to withdraw and smash back into the paradise she offered. Caroline deserved every ounce of his self-control.

"You fit," she whispered in wonder.

Her tone brought a smile to his lips. Damn, this woman was dangerous. Hot, enchanting, and addictive. "Let's see how good we can make this, Precious. Hold on."

Fighting for control, Wraith focused on making this unforgettable for her. He searched for the best angle. When she clutched him tighter, Wraith focused his efforts there. Her small sounds drove him crazy. He wanted this to last as long as possible.

The room heated around them as they moved against each other. Wraith loved the taste of her salty skin. He brushed her thick hair away and tugged her head back to claim her lips. That small touch of pain increased Caroline's movements. Her hands slid down his spine to grip his butt as she ground herself against him. Her cry of delight echoed around him.

Three.

Finally, Wraith quickened his pace. He drove deep into her and treasured how she met each of his thrusts. Feeling his climax gathering, Wraith was determined to get her there as well. He slid a hand between their bodies to tap her clit. Wraith growled, "Come with me, Precious."

"I can't," she protested.

"You can. One more time, Little girl," he encouraged and nuzzled that sensitive spot where her neck and shoulder met. Kissing her skin, Wraith then closed his mouth around her. He bit down gently, giving her another taste of pain.

"Ahhhhh!" Her scream ricocheted off the empty walls.

Pounding into her, Wraith allowed himself to join her orgasm.

Four.

When their thudding hearts slowed, Wraith maneuvered them under the covers and gathered Caroline to his chest. He'd break it to her tomorrow that her wild one-night stand had morphed into something much more permanent.

Heat wrapped around Caroline, feeling like heaven. She blinked her eyes open and stared at the alarm clock. 8:32 a.m. How long had it been since she'd slept in?

Caroline smirked. Okay, she hadn't slept very much last night. Did lovers like Wraith actually exist? Those who acted like you were the sexiest woman on earth?

She inhaled deeply. His male scent filled her senses. She'd never forget the aroma of hot, sexy man. *Biker,* she corrected herself.

Shifting slightly, she bit her lip to stifle a moan. Had she ever been sore after sex? Wraith had taken such tender care of her, but he was huge. *And so good.* She smirked.

"I'd love to hear what's going on in that mind of yours, Precious." His deep voice rumbled over her. That bass tone would replay in her fantasies for years to come. Why was she sure all her heroes from now on would have low voices?

A million dollars couldn't convince her to share those thoughts. Caroline turned in his arms and pressed a light smooch to those amazing lips that had kissed nearly every inch of her body last night. "I had a really good time last night. You're something special."

"I enjoyed myself as well," he told her with a smile before leaning forward to kiss her. The exchange caught fire quickly.

She pulled back reluctantly. "I don't think I can take any more," she whispered.

His slow, knowing wink made Caroline duck her head as her face heated. She suspected she was turning a vivid shade of red. Firm fingers lifted her chin.

When their gazes met, he said softly, "Best damn night ever. And I always want you to tell me how you really feel. Did I hurt you?"

"Never. It's just...." her voice trailed off. How did she share he was twice the size Adam was?

"Take a warm bath, Little girl."

His stern tone did something to her inside. He was such a Daddy. She wished this could be more. Now that she'd had a glimpse of what sex could be like, Caroline would compare everyone to her one night with Wraith. Sadness filled her. Life was so unfair. If only things could be different and Wraith would want to stick around.

"You haven't figured it out yet, have you?" he asked slowly.

"Figured what out?" she wondered, confused.

"I'm not going anywhere. Do you have time for breakfast, Precious?"

She stared at him. Did he mean today? She decided to address the second question. "I can make pancakes."

"I'll make pancakes. Do you like puppies or kitties better?"

"Kitties?" she chose one, feeling clueless. What was he talking about?

"Go soak. I'll make the bed and then go raid your kitchen. Kitten pancakes coming up."

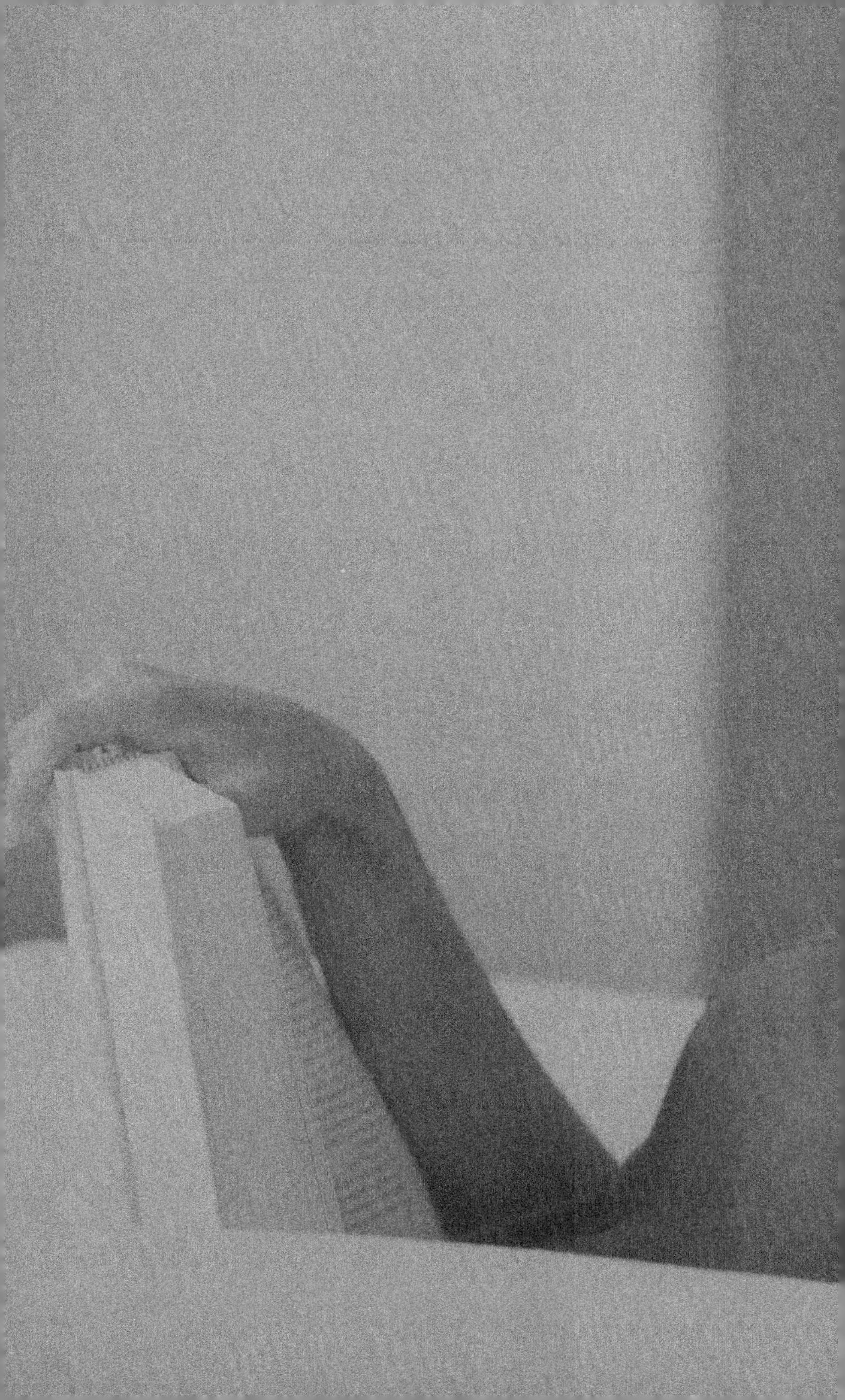

CHAPTER 5

Caroline glared at her computer and tried to see anything other than the adorable kitten pancakes Wraith had created for her. She still had a few carefully wrapped in plastic and stowed in her freezer. She'd saved them when he was busy loading her sink full of dirty dishes into the dishwasher along with their breakfast things.

He did dishes. Automatically. Like without her even asking. Who was this man?

He'd also made it crystal clear that they were now a thing, and he planned to see her often. According to Wraith, a Daddy didn't walk away from a Little who enchanted them. She'd repeated that phrase to herself several times and even typed it into her document by mistake.

The kiss he'd given her on the way out the door had sizzled so much she'd had to squash the temptation to head back to the bedroom to use her vibrator—but that had felt like cheating on him. Caroline sensed he wouldn't like that. She might have earned another spanking.

Crap! She was going to have to change her panties.

"Think of anything else," she told herself sternly. "Write something."

Putting her fingers on the keys, she started outlining a story. Using the research she'd gathered at the bar last night, Caroline created biker characters for her fictional club. She searched for tough names, and Google gave her some excellent suggestions. None seemed as sexy as Wraith, but she liked several. Those would do.

When she was straining her eyes to see, Caroline glanced away from her computer and discovered the room was full of shadows. She'd written the entire day. Stretching, she groaned. Her already sore body was now stiff from sitting in one spot for hours. Time to stop.

After carefully saving her document in three places, Caroline stood. She grabbed the insulated tumbler she had drained hours ago and headed to get something to eat with a satisfied smile. This book, hell, this series was going to be amazing.

Caroline poured herself a glass of tea from her refrigerator and grabbed her phone. She never took it into her office while she was writing. It was too distracting. Besides, no one other than scam artists called her, anyway.

She opened it and saw a message. *Driveway. Mailbox.*

Walking to the front window, she spotted her car parked in her driveway. She'd totally forgotten about it in the parking lot at Inferno. Wraith had delivered it to her without a word. Hurrying down her stairs, she zipped out the front door and checked the mailbox affixed to the siding. Her keys.

Caroline hugged them to her chest as she turned and walked back inside. Closing the door, she leaned against it as her mind whirled a million miles a minute. She didn't want this to be a one-night stand. Had he really meant it when he'd said that earlier? How did she tell him that's what she wanted now too?

Grabbing her phone from the stretchy pocket on her leggings, Caroline sent him a message. It only took about fifteen minutes and lots of revisions to figure out what to say. In the end, she went with a simple message.

. . .

Thank you.

Immediately, her phone buzzed with a response.
I wanted you to have wheels to come see me.
Tonight?
Caroline's pulse increased at the thought of seeing him so quickly.
Good idea. See you soon, Precious. I'm at the back bar. Drive carefully.

Caroline flew into the closet, searching for something special to wear. She pushed the hangers across the rod, rejecting almost everything as too tight, too ugly, too outdated, or too uptight. She settled on a fitted dress with a moderate neckline and a denim vest. It would have to do.

Tossing those on the bed, she ran to the bathroom to put on makeup. Caroline never wore very much. She considered intensifying her look but was afraid to transform herself into a clown. Wraith had pursued her last night without all that gunk. She crossed her fingers, hoping he hadn't changed his mind.

While she'd worked late for her, Caroline suspected that Inferno would just be starting to rock now. When she was dressed, Caroline grabbed her purse and keys. She was so nervous she almost forgot to put down the garage door. After forcing herself to stop and take a couple of deep breaths, Caroline got on the road.

So many motorcycles filled the lot tonight. Every time she thought she'd found an empty parking space, Caroline discovered a bike backed into it. She finally drove to the back of the lot and grabbed a spot there.

Wraith wasn't on door duty when she walked in. The guy's cut reminded Caroline she'd heard the name before. "Oh, Scythe, you helped with my ex last night. Thank you."

He gave her a strange look before glancing at her ID. "Caroline. No problem. He's a jerk. Wraith's working at the back bar." He pointed toward the far wall. "Go that way and circle the room to the far wall. It will take you to the right place."

"Thank you, Scythe." Darting inside, she followed Scythe's directions. The slightly younger man was definitely handsome. They all had muscles on top of muscles. Was that a requirement to join the Devil Daddies MC?

"Devil Daddies." Caroline repeated that name to herself, and pieces of a puzzle clicked together. They couldn't all be Daddies, could they?

"Whoa, Precious. You almost wiped out that server." Wraith caught her with one arm and steadied the tray for the employee as well.

"Oh, I'm so sorry," Caroline said to the server, feeling embarrassed that her distraction had almost caused a disaster.

"My dodge game must be off today. No problem," the relieved waitress answered and darted away to deliver the drinks.

"I am such a klutz," Caroline admitted and then stared at Wraith when the memory of his punishment crossed her mind. Heat flared under her fitted dress. "You can't spank me here!" she hissed.

"Don't speak poorly about yourself, then."

Studying his stern face, Caroline guessed she didn't have a chance in hell to change his mind. So, she changed tactics and wrapped her arms around his neck. Bouncing up on her tiptoes, she kissed him hard.

Caroline's mind was fuzzy when he let her go. Wraith had taken immediate control of that kiss, and it had almost gotten out of hand. His touch made her forget where she was. Her urge to climb him in public wouldn't be acceptable even at Inferno. She appreciated his steady hands at her waist.

"Wow," she whispered.

"Hi, Precious. I've missed you."

"I missed you too."

"Wraith! We need you, brother!" a biker called him from behind the bar.

"On it," Wraith answered back and urged Caroline to an occupied stool at the counter.

"Out," he ordered. The man got up without question and ambled off into the crowd.

"That was rude," Caroline hissed as he helped her onto the warm stool.

"Bad biker dude, right?" he reminded her before moving behind the bar.

In a few minutes, he'd pulled enough beers to catch the bartenders up and was concocting fancy shots for a rowdy bridal shower party. When he pushed one toward Caroline, she shook her head.

"I'm a total wimp."

Wraith poured the shot into a glass and added something from a dispenser behind the bar. "Sip on that." With his eyes on her, he loaded the order onto a tray as the women cheered him on.

"Wraith's yours?" a flashy blonde demanded.

Without hesitating, Caroline answered, "Yes. I'm in my bad boy era." As she suspected, that was the perfect way to change the more than slightly intoxicated celebrators' attitudes.

"Hell, yeah! I need to dive into my own bad boy," a brunette chimed in.

"Or have him dive into you," the bride suggested, drawing peals of laughter and hoots from the women.

To Caroline's relief, they dashed to the dance floor when a popular song filled the bar. She glanced back at Wraith, who hummed the bad boy jingle under his breath as he worked on the next order.

"What was I supposed to say?" Caroline raised her shoulders and shrugged.

"I liked your answer, Little girl."

Oh! She'd claimed him. "We suck at one-night stands," she pointed out lightly.

"We do. I'm good with that." Wraith told her.

"It's a boy!" rang through the PA system.

"Did someone just have a baby? Here?" Caroline asked.

"Belinda." A server with Amy on her nametag appeared next to her. "Her water broke behind the bar. Razor drove her to the hospital while Wraith and Toxin jumped in to clean before taking her spot."

"She worked until her water broke?" Caroline said in amazement. That was tough.

"Yeah. She wanted all her maternity leave with her baby," Amy answered as she maneuvered the tray of drinks onto her shoulder.

"Introduce me, Wraith," a raspy voice demanded.

"Lucien, this is my girl, Caroline. Caroline, this is the President of the Devil Daddies MC, Inferno's owner, and my boss." Wraith easily listed off his positions.

"Hi. It's nice to meet you," Caroline said politely to the hard-looking man with a ton of tattoos. Did that cross mean Lucien had been in prison or maybe he'd killed someone? She hoped she didn't move when a shiver ran down her spine. He looked lethal.

"That's the first time anyone has called me nice," Lucien said with a skeptical expression. He stared at Caroline, frightening her.

"Mine, Lucien. She meant nothing by it." Wraith stood up for her as he continued to pour drinks. He didn't seem bothered by Lucien's attitude.

"Got it. Enjoy your time at Inferno, Caroline."

She slumped with relief when the scary man walked away. Okay, she was wrong. They couldn't all be Daddies.

"Lucien is a shrewd businessman, Caroline," Wraith said before changing the subject. "Tell me what you did today."

"I got a lot done at work," she answered. For some reason,

she hesitated to tell him she was an author. Caroline didn't want him to think she was hanging around to gather information.

A small voice in the back of her mind reminded her that was exactly what she was doing. Caroline pushed that from her thoughts and concentrated on Wraith.

"How long have you been a bartender? I thought you manned the door."

"The club members pitch in here when they want to. This is our MC's hangout place. Lucien opens it up to the public as a community outreach. Many people come here because it feels thrilling."

Caroline nodded. She could understand that. She controlled her expression as she dared to ask, "What's your MC position? Vice-President?"

"I'm the Enforcer."

"That sounds mean. You're the one who beats people up?" she asked, appalled.

"Only when they deserve it," Wraith answered as if it were a joke. "I need to run to the back for some vodka. Stay there for me, okay?"

Caroline struggled to find something to say, so she nodded. No one in her life used physical violence to solve problems. Suddenly, she didn't think she could do this. They were from two entirely different worlds.

When Wraith's broad shoulders disappeared through a swinging door, Caroline scrambled off the stool.

"Hey, Caroline, isn't it? Wraith will be right back. He wants you to stay there," the other bartender reminded her.

Frantically, she came up with an excuse. "I... I'm just going to the bathroom."

"I'll keep your seat available." Immediately, a man tried to claim it as Caroline stepped away, and the other bartender interjected. "Hey, that seat's taken. Go sit somewhere else."

"She got up," the man argued.

"That's Wraith's girl. Do you want to mess with him?"

The color leached out of the would-be chair thief's face. He faded into the crowd.

Quickly, Caroline executed her own disappearing act. When she neared the door, she saw Scythe answer his phone. Sure that Wraith knew what she was doing, Caroline turned to dart down a hallway. She didn't really understand why this felt so wrong suddenly. How could she explain it to Wraith? Reaching a door at the end, she rattled the doorknob. Locked.

"Caroline?"

Slowly, she turned to see the leader of the MC and panicked inside. "Lucien. I was going to get a breath of fresh air."

"Wraith will be here in a minute," he told her. Did he look disappointed in Caroline?

Wraith's voice came from her right. "I'm here, Lucien. Thanks, brother."

Lucien faded away, leaving them alone.

"I'll walk you out to your car if that's your destination," Wraith told her.

"I was just going to get some fresh...."

"Don't lie to me, Caroline. I'll see you safely to your ride."

He knew. She swallowed hard, feeling terrible. "You don't have to."

"I do. Come on."

Wraith pulled a loaded keyring from his pocket and deftly located the key. Unlocking the door she'd tried to open, he ushered Caroline through. Once outside, he locked it behind them. "Where'd you park?"

Caroline waved a hand in the general direction.

"Lead the way," he instructed. Wraith fell in step next to her as she walked.

Searching for anything to say, Caroline's heart broke. His face was expressionless. For the first time, she couldn't read him at all. She couldn't see any trace of the playful Daddy who'd made her pancakes or the intense lover who'd rocked her world. "I'm sorry...."

He cut her off. "That's too easy to say. You're running away from something that could be magical, and I have to watch you do it."

"Wraith," she tried when they reached her car.

"I won't bother you, Caroline. Have a great life." Wraith stepped back and waited a car distance from her as she slid into her car and started it.

How she maneuvered her car out of the parking spot, Caroline didn't have a clue. She drove by instinct. Her brain whirled with the argument of whether she'd done the smartest or stupidest thing in the world.

Walking into her house, Caroline gave into the tears that had threatened since she'd seen Wraith's deadpan face in the hall. He'd hidden his emotions from her for the first time. She'd hurt him badly. She wrapped her arms around her torso and threw herself on the couch. Tears coursed down her cheeks until she was completely empty inside.

Adam had ripped her heart to shreds by not caring about her. She couldn't risk giving her heart to someone from the wrong side of the law. Violence made her ill. It went against every value her parents had drilled into her. Caroline knew without asking Wraith couldn't change who he was. How could she think she could fall in love with a bad boy?

CHAPTER 6

The End.

Caroline stared at those two simple words. It had taken her six weeks to write and rewrite her first motorcycle club romance. She loved the grit and emotion that had woven its way through the story. Caroline didn't think she'd done it alone.

The magic had happened, along with so many anguished moments. Some days, she'd struggled to read the words she typed—her vision blurred by the tears that cascaded down her cheeks as she immersed herself in the two characters. Deep inside, Caroline understood this was the best book she'd ever crafted. She had a hunch her editor would agree. Before she could second-guess her decision that the story was perfected, Caroline sent it off.

Pushing her chair away from her desk, she glanced out the window. The light green spring leaves had matured, and the sun blazed. Caroline had survived every single day that passed. The hole in her heart hadn't repaired itself. She could still feel Wraith's arms around her.

She'd tried to go see him at Inferno. Scythe had turned her away at the door. His harsh expression had softened a bit when she'd burst into tears. Horrified by losing her control, Caroline had fled past all the bar goers lined up to get in. She'd dressed up twice to visit again and hadn't made it out of her garage. Pride hadn't held her back. A picture of Wraith's face flashed on repeat in her mind. He didn't want to see her.

Brushing the tears from her cheeks, she stood and walked purposefully into her bathroom. After washing her face, Caroline pulled on a comfortable pair of jeans and her favorite fuchsia top. Maybe it would bolster her confidence. After applying a scant amount of makeup, she grabbed her keys and courage on the way out the door.

At three in the afternoon, no one stood at the front entrance. Caroline walked in and scanned the room. A few people sat at the bar, getting an early start. Caroline headed for a stool.

"What can I get you?"

"Wraith and a diet cola, please."

"He's pretty potent by himself," the young woman said with a smile as she dispensed the drink. "I don't think Wraith is here yet. I'll call up to the office to see."

"He's not."

The flat voice made Caroline turn. Scythe's expression was hard and remote. She ignored it and forced herself to say, "Hi, Scythe. I'll wait."

"He doesn't want to see you."

"I know. I want to see him enough for both of us."

"Your drink is on the house. Leave now," Scythe ordered.

"I'm not going. I'll stay until Wraith arrives," Caroline told him softly. "Please, Scythe. I need to talk to him."

The biker crossed his arms, displaying his massive biceps as he stared her down. Caroline swallowed hard but didn't waver. This would be the last time she approached him. If he refused, there was no chance for her to make this right.

Grabbing the last of her courage and shredding her pride, Caroline whispered, "I'm his Little girl, Scythe. I screwed up. I have to see if I can fix this. Help me, please."

He blinked.

Caroline counted three full breaths as she waited for his decision. She blinked furiously to hold back the tears that prickled the inside of her eyelids away and crossed her fingers on both hands.

"He's at the warehouse in back. Go through the rear door. At the gate, tell them I sent you to Wraith. They'll let you in."

She slid off her stool and grabbed a ten from her pocket to set on the bar. "Thank you, Scythe. I owe you one."

Before he could change his mind or stop her, she hurried through the bar and burst through the door marked Authorized Personnel Only. Bikers leaned against the wall with a bottle of beer. They all turned to check her out. Caroline didn't pause but nodded and kept going toward the tall concrete walls, topped with razor wire. Scythe's name worked like a charm at the gate. They handed her a visitor's hard hat and sent her inside to building two.

Steadying the unfamiliar weight on her head, Caroline scanned the wide space. Spotting a large yellow two on a massive building to her right, Caroline started walking. Men zipped by on all sorts of heavy-moving equipment. The forklifts were laden with huge packing crates.

She wanted to hesitate at the door but forced herself to enter. Inside, a wide set of shoulders drew her attention. Caroline headed toward the familiar figure, completely focused on reaching him.

A loud horn burst, and a squeal of brakes behind her made Caroline jump. Whirling around, she met the gaze of the driver, who looked completely pissed. "I'm sorry!"

"You're going to get yourself killed, lady. Get out of here," he yelled, half hanging out of the window.

"Enough. She's with me." Wraith's gravelly voice came from beside her. He stepped between Caroline and the irate driver.

"Sorry, Wraith. Keep her out of the driving lane," The man grumped before moving on.

Caroline held her breath as Wraith slowly turned to face her. He wrapped an arm around her waist and steered her to the side. The heat of his touch made her ache inside. When he removed his hand, her heart sank. A tear escaped and tumbled down her cheek. Quickly, she dashed it away.

"Thank you, Wraith."

"Why are you here? It's not safe," he growled.

"I needed to see you. You wouldn't respond to my texts, and the guys at the door wouldn't let me into Inferno," she said, wringing her hands in front of her as she searched for the right thing to say.

"Sounds like you should have put the pieces together and moved on."

"I got scared, Wraith. I was stupid. Can we talk, please?"

"Talking is overrated. You were attracted to the bad guy from the wrong side of town. You got fucked well and then decided I didn't fit into your life."

"Wraith, it wasn't like that," she protested. She had to make him understand.

"Then tell me your version."

"You turned my world upside down," she said. When his mouth curled downward even more, Caroline rushed to say, "In a marvelous way. I was excited. No, more than excited. No one ever treated me like you did. Like I was special."

"Then you're hanging out with the wrong people, Caroline." His voice held no emotion. It was completely flat.

"I agree. I recently divorced after five years of hell. He checked off all the boxes that I thought were what I needed. I was so wrong."

"We're not solving anything here, Caroline. Go back home. Have a good, safe life. You'll have a story to tell your grandchildren about your night on the wild side."

"No."

He shrugged those broad shoulders and looked at her like she had lost her mind. "What do you mean, no?"

Gathering her courage, Caroline stepped so close her body touched his. She grabbed his shirt as tightly as she could to hold on. "No. I'm not leaving. I won't. It was a mistake to run away before. I won't do it again."

Wraith pulled off his hard hat and ran his fingers through his thick hair. "Caroline, it's okay. I understand."

"But you don't. I met a man unlike anyone else. He stepped right out of my fantasies. But he was real."

"Fantasies and real life are very different."

"Could you forgive me for panicking? Please." Caroline begged.

Wraith took a half step back, and Caroline moved with him. She wouldn't let him get away without a fight.

"Okay, Caroline. I forgive you. Is that what you need to hear?"

"No. I need you to call me Precious. To hug me. Maybe spank my bottom for how I acted. I need you to not just say the words. I need you to mean them."

He closed his eyes for several seconds before reopening them to stare back down at her. Shaking his head as if rebuking himself, Wraith wrapped his hands around her waist and asked, "What scared you?"

"The Enforcer thing. I've never known anyone who exists to be violent."

"You've watched too many movies. I don't go around beating people up or worse. An Enforcer's job contains muscle, but most of it is using this muscle," Wraith pointed to his head. "I handle disputes between members and make sure everyone is following the rules."

"So, you're like a police officer."

"I guess you could look at it that way if you'd rather. I'm not going to lie to you. The Devil Daddies will use force if it's warranted without a second thought."

She swallowed hard and forced herself to ask, "Does that include you?"

"Yes."

He didn't explain. Caroline understood he wouldn't. "I guess what's really important is…. Do you still care about me, Wraith, or did I ruin everything?"

Wraith studied her face. Was he debating how he felt or trying to figure out if he could trust her?

He lifted a hand and cupped her jaw, threading his fingers through her hair. Seconds ticked by, as she waited for him to decide. When he shook his head, she inhaled sharply and expected the worst.

"Damn, I've missed you."

The tears she'd worked so hard to hold back poured down her cheeks. "I've missed you too."

"We don't do this again, Precious. Don't leave me without giving us time to talk things over."

"I won't run away. I knew I was stupid before I reached the car."

"Don't call yourself stupid, Little girl," he told her as he wiped her tears from her cheeks with calloused hands.

"Wraith? You done? We need you over here." A voice yelled from the end of the aisle.

"Fuck off, Fury," Wraith answered without glancing away from her.

"I'll find Vex to help," the biker called back.

"I don't want to get you in trouble," Caroline whispered.

"You won't. Vex will handle it until I show up. I've got something urgent going on now. It's going to take a while. Can you wait for me?"

"Definitely. Shall I go back to the bar?" she asked.

"If anyone bothers you, tell them Wraith said Code Pink."

"Code Pink," she repeated so she wouldn't forget it. Caroline hesitated for a split second before daring to ask, "Could you kiss me?"

Wraith claimed her lips with a soft, sweet kiss. It didn't

contain the heat she craved but soothed her heart. He cared about her.

Smiling, Caroline released his shirt. She'd hold on later. "Thank you for giving me another chance."

"Go wash your face, Little girl. No more tears. I'll be there soon," he promised.

After retracing her steps, Caroline handed the hard hat back to the men at the door with her thanks. They didn't ask her questions, but she could tell they'd spotted her blotchy face. She smiled to reassure them everything was okay before returning to Inferno.

"I didn't get a call to escort you off the grounds," Scythe greeted her as she practically skipped inside. He rose from his lean against the wall.

"No. I'm going to wait for Wraith in the bar," Caroline told him, unsure what to say. "Thank you for helping me."

"Call if you need something. I'm around."

The handsome biker strode away without another word. Guessing she must have passed some test with him, Caroline headed to the bathroom to erase the tear marks from her face. She wanted to look her best for Wraith.

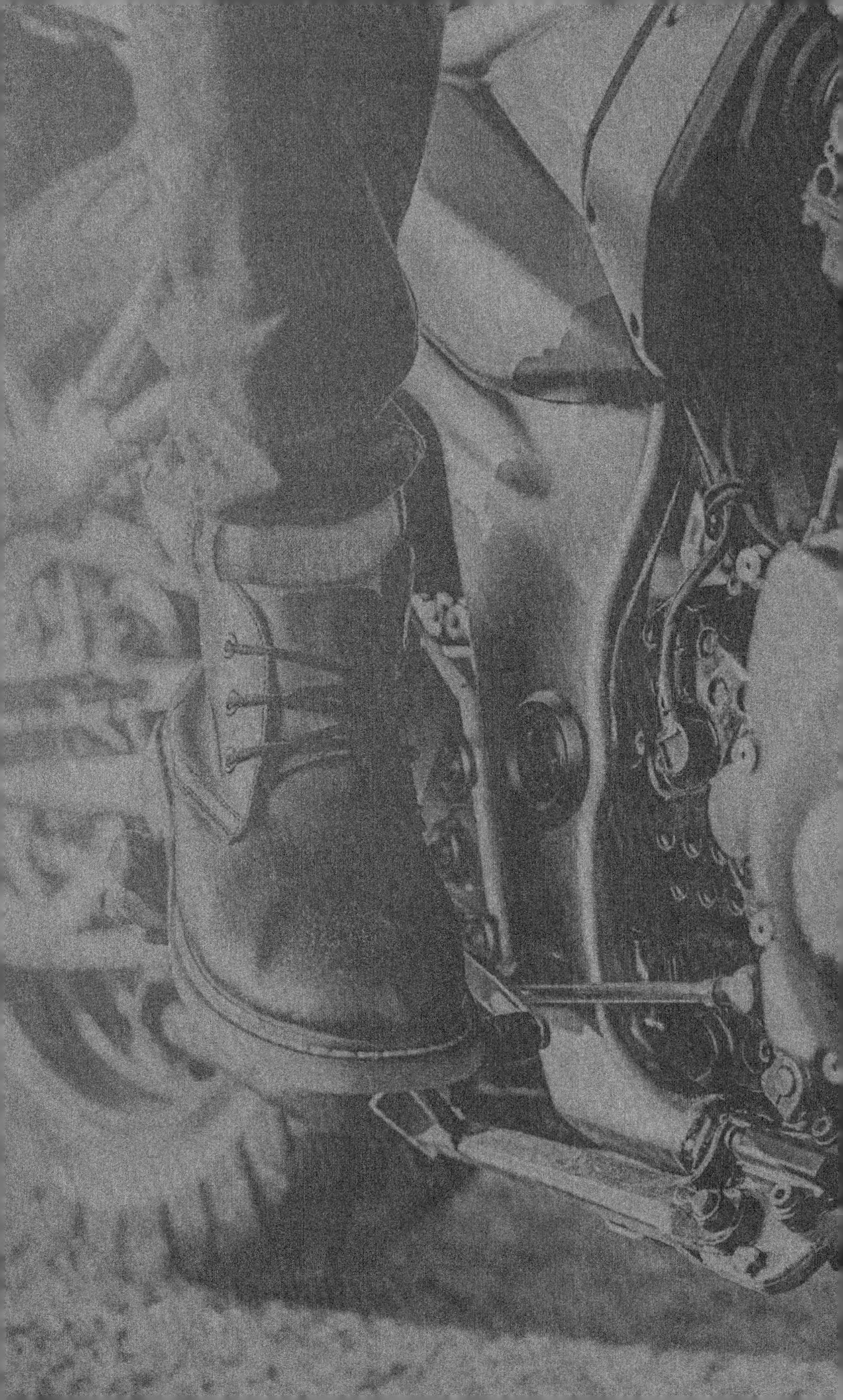

CHAPTER 7

Wraith spotted Caroline at the bar and headed her way. As much as he loved hanging out at Inferno, he was eager to have her all to himself. Scoping out the area, he spotted Scythe stationed near the bar, keeping an eye on her. He paused when he got close to the other biker.

"You sent her?" Wraith asked.

"You've been a complete ass for weeks. I figured that meant something," Scythe answered.

"Yeah. Thanks. I owe you one."

"Hopefully, I'll get to collect someday. I have to find my Little first."

"My fingers are crossed for you. I'm out tonight," Wraith told him.

"Lucien already found a replacement," Scythe shared with a grin.

"You talked to Lucien?"

"Nah. Lucien is aware of everything that happens on his turf. I saw the assignments update an hour ago. Take a few days away," Scythe suggested.

"I'll do that."

Without another word, Wraith continued toward the special

woman at the bar. He'd wanted to go claim her a hundred times over the last few weeks but knew Caroline would have to decide to accept him as he was. As the days had stretched on, he'd lost hope. When he'd turned around to find her looking adorable in that hard hat, he'd been shocked. He'd had to lock himself in place to keep from hugging her.

He placed a hand on the small of her back. "Let's get out of here," he stated firmly.

"I've kept a good eye on her, Wraith," the cheerful bartender said.

"Thanks, Sherry. I owe you one," Wraith told her as Caroline slid from the stool to stand next to him. He pulled his money clip from his pocket and peeled off a twenty. "Does this cover her tab?"

"Way over," Sherry said, waving away his payment. "I've enjoyed getting to chat with Caroline."

Wraith placed the bill on the counter for her. "Have a good evening, Sherry."

Turning, he wrapped his arm around Caroline and guided her to the door. "Where's your car?"

Caroline waved a hand vaguely around the parking lot. "I don't remember. I wasn't thinking too well when I came in."

"Let's go find it." He steered her toward the same side she'd chosen last time. Most people followed a pattern. "Are you hungry, Caroline?"

"I could eat," she shared, staring up at him. "Wraith, I'm really sorry."

"No more apologies, Little girl."

"But...."

He interrupted her, "We both made mistakes. I don't plan on letting anything get between us again."

Caroline nodded and put her arm around his waist. "I missed you so much. I haven't changed my sheets. They stopped smelling like you a couple of weeks ago."

Her sweet confession went straight to his gut. Thank goodness she'd come to him. Wraith had driven to her condo several times before veering off track. Scaring her wasn't an option.

"I've missed you too. Will you come home with me, Precious?"

"I'd like that. Oh! There's my car," she said, pointing ahead.

Wraith made a mental note to put a tracker in her car. Then, he'd be able to find it for her easily. "Wait for me to pull up over there and then back out to follow me. Drive carefully. The guard will take pictures and need to see your driver's license."

He hugged her close and kissed her hard, claiming her as his To his delight, she rose on her tiptoes to get closer to him, looping her arms around his neck. When he lifted his head, she made a quiet sound of protest that went straight to his cock. Pushing the temptation to kiss her away, Wraith forced himself to step back.

"I'll go slow so you don't lose me. My house is close but down a country road from here," he warned before jogging to his bike.

In a few minutes, they were on their way. Wraith took the road that circled behind Inferno and the warehouses. The fence line surrounding the latter went deep into the woods.

Lucien had invested in a ton of land when he'd decided to open the bar. Already, the MC leader had built an additional warehouse to expand. No one, other than the Devil Daddies, was aware of this settlement. He approached the gate and waited for Caroline to pull in behind him.

"Pirate, this is Caroline. She's mine. Let her in when she comes," Wraith told him.

Pirate nodded and snapped a quick picture of the front of his Little's car, including the license plate. He'd take another picture of her and her license when she reached him. "Congrats."

Wraith advanced a bit more and let Pirate finish adding Caroline to the approved list. When the biker on duty glanced back at him and waved, Wraith drove into the complex and headed for his cabin. It was quiet now. Most of the members were rolling into Inferno for an evening of fun. A few of his brothers were in camp, of course. They'd worked overnight shifts and were recharging.

Trying to see the place through her eyes, Wraith studied the complex. It reminded him more of a campground than a biker hangout. Sure, the Devils had bikes parked in different places and a big repair shop close to the entrance, but gigantic trees arched over the paved roads shading the wooden cabins they passed, giving the complex a tranquil feel. Strands of white, round bulbs illuminated the paths at night. Rustic and peaceful—it was an oasis hidden from view.

He pulled into his driveway and triggered the garage. After stashing his bike at the side of the large space, he waved Caroline to pull in next to him. He grabbed a remote from the drawer in his workbench and quickly added a tracking device to the clip. Walking to the driver's door, he handed the device to her.

"Put this in your glove box. You hit the big button to raise and lower the door," he told her.

"Oh, I won't come here without you," she promised, hesitating to follow his directions.

"This is safe ground. You are welcome any time. Go ahead. Put it in your glove box." After she'd followed his directions, he opened her door and helped her slide out of the driver's seat.

"Is that why that guy took pictures of me and my car?"

"Yes. Visitors are allowed only if a Devil has vouched for them."

"This is your place?" she asked, looking around the neat garage.

"It is. Come in, Caroline. Let me make you some dinner and we'll talk," Wraith suggested.

"I'd like that, but I can help."

"Not going to happen, Little girl. Daddy cooks," he told her bluntly. She needed to understand from the beginning that he was in charge. Especially in his home.

"Okay. Maybe you'd let me set the table?"

"I think I could be sweet-talked into that."

He led her out of the garage and to the front door. After twisting the knob, he pushed the door open. Wraith turned to Caroline and swept her off her feet. Before she could protest, he carried her into his home. He closed the door with his elbow before walking to his favorite chair.

"Wraith, I'm not a bride," she said in surprise.

"You are the first woman I've brought home," Wraith told her as he sat down.

"Really? How long have you lived here?"

"Three years."

He loved the shock on her face. "What?" Her elbow struck him sharply in the ribs as she struggled to sit up straight. In self-preservation, Wraith wrapped his hands around her waist to boost her into position.

Caroline stared at him. "You haven't had anyone in your house for three years?"

"I've had sex in that time period, Precious. I haven't brought them to my cabin."

"Why not?"

"The Devils decided when this compound first went in that we weren't using it as a hotel. This is our home. Everyone is welcome to bring someone important here, but it's not the place for flings."

"I'm not a fling?" she asked.

"You are not. You're my Little girl."

"I can't believe I screwed this up so badly," she whispered.

"You were very brave to come to Inferno today. Crafty too, since you'd visited before."

"You were aware I'd been there and let them turn me away?"

"Yes. Were you ready then to take me as I am?" he asked, studying her expression.

"Yes. Well, probably."

"I wanted you to be happy, Caroline. It seemed obvious that

having me in your life would create tension and problems. I didn't want that for you," he told her.

"But you were unhappy."

"Yes."

"You were going to let me go, so I'd be… happy?" she asked and then shook her head. "I think we both deserve to enjoy life."

"Let's set that as our goal. Now, I'm grilling steaks for dinner. How do you like yours cooked?"

"Medium rare."

"The best way to make a steak. Now, mac and cheese or potatoes?"

"I love mac and cheese but only the kind in the blue box."

"You'll try my homemade dish soon, but I have a box stashed in my pantry," Wraith admitted.

"Can I have a tour of your house?"

He immediately shook his head. "Too much temptation. Wander anywhere you wish, Precious. I'm not going to step a foot into any room with a bed with you until you're fed."

"We could skip…."

"Did you eat breakfast and lunch?" he asked sharply.

"No," Caroline admitted.

"Dinner first. Go explore. I'll get the grill fired up and the water boiling."

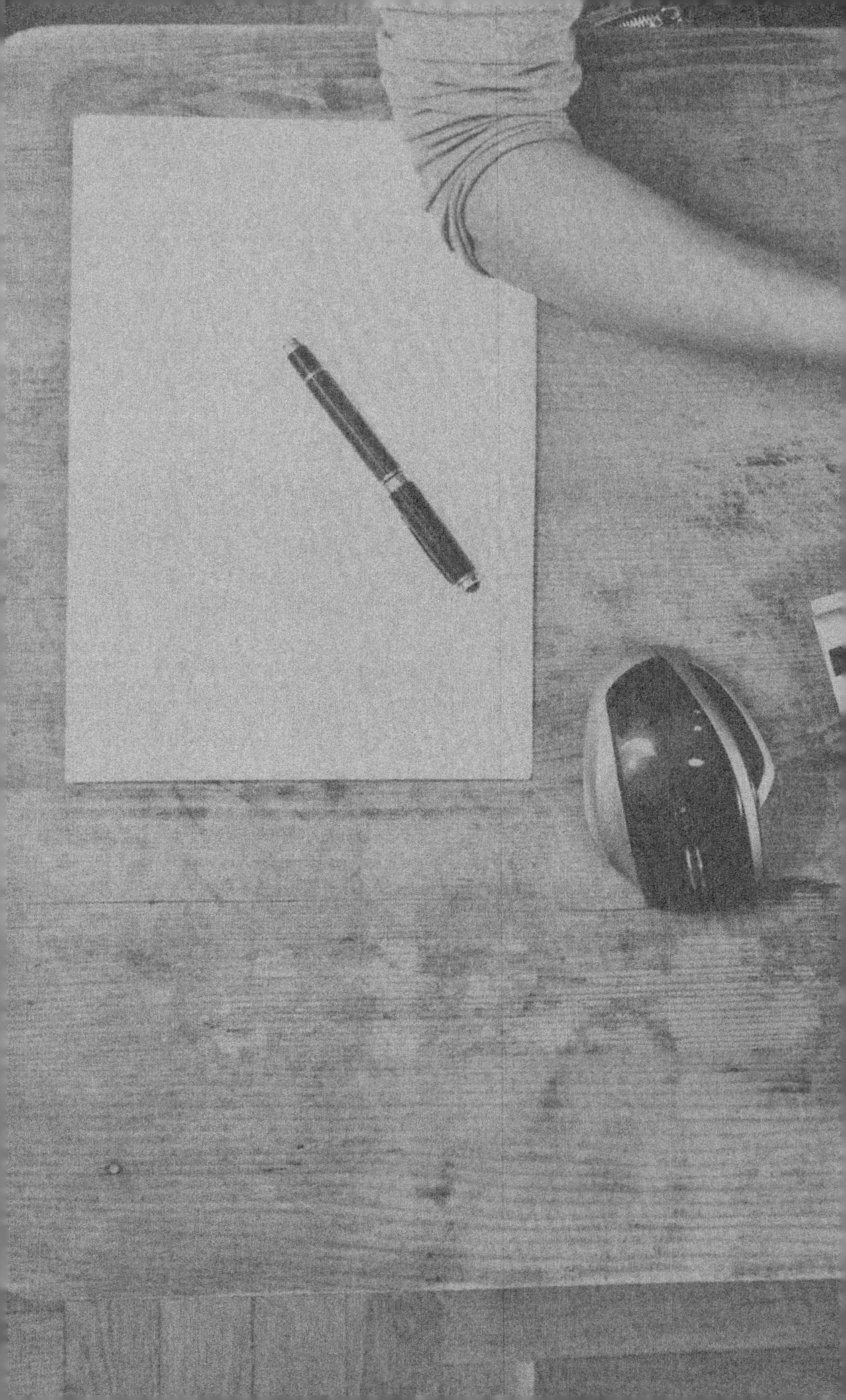

CHAPTER 8

When Wraith moved into the kitchen, Caroline checked out the room. The chair they'd sat in was obviously his favorite. Oversized and heavily padded, it had welcomed her like an old friend. Next to it sat a thick spy thriller on a handy end table with a lamp. She smiled at the thought of Wraith reading in a pool of light. He was definitely so much more than she'd expected from a biker.

Something was missing. She scanned the family room again. A bookshelf full of reading material stood against the far wall. Wait!

"You don't have a TV?"

"Nope."

"How do you watch movies?" she asked.

"I drive to the theatre and buy popcorn," he answered.

"They do have the best popcorn. But what about for videos?"

"Do you have some favorite movies?"

"Sure. I think I've watched a few special ones forty times or more," Caroline admitted.

"Then we make a blanket fort and watch on my laptop," Wraith suggested.

"That would be fun." She didn't really care about keeping up with the news. It was always sad things, anyway. She checked out the room, debating whether she should roam through Wraith's house alone. She had his permission. Wandering over to the bookshelf, she perused his books. Several looked interesting to devour on her own. Others she hoped he'd read to her. The thought of listening to that gravelly voice narrating a story sounded yummy.

When Wraith disappeared outside to start the grill, her curiosity made her dart down the hall. She stopped at the first door. An enormous hole pierced through the hollow door. Caroline peered through it to see a pink room inside.

Who did it belong to? And why had Wraith put his fist through the door? She turned the doorknob. Locked.

As she rattled it, a small piece of metal fell from the wooden head jam. Caroline bent to pick it up and discovered the metal device fit into the hole in the lock to open it. Before she could talk herself out of it, she pressed it into place, and the door clicked open.

Caroline couldn't believe her eyes. Wraith had created a beautiful nursery for an adult Little girl. The walls were a soft pink with varying sizes of white hearts scattered here and there for decoration. The white wood of the furniture matched, giving the room additional charm.

She walked forward to run her hand over the railing of the oversized crib. Her fingers came away dusty. No one had been in here for a while. Or was it that he hadn't dusted in the nursery for a few weeks? She focused back on the hole in the door. Caroline suspected when that had happened. Tears filled her eyes.

"I didn't have time to replace the door, Little girl. You surprised me today."

Caroline whirled around to stare at Wraith, who leaned against the doorframe. "You made this for your Little girl before you found her."

"I did. I wanted to be ready when she appeared," he said, moving forward to take her into his arms. "Don't cry, Precious.

Maybe we shouldn't play in this space for a few days. Let me get it cleaned up and ready for you."

"I love this room. It's straight out of my fantasies. I don't care that it's dusty."

"I hope you'll love it for many years to come," he told her softly.

"I know I'm not supposed to apologize anymore, but...."

"You weren't ready. That's okay. Better to run away and come back when you made up your mind—once—than to get involved in something you don't want. Notice, I said once. My heart can't take you leaving anymore, Caroline. Talk to me if doubts creep into your mind. Perhaps together, we can work out whatever is scaring you. Can you make me that promise, Little girl?"

Caroline nodded yes and stepped closer to Wraith to press her cheek to his broad chest. He smelled like charcoal and fire. Those scents reassured her that this was real, not one of the many dreams she'd woken up from and cried to discover she'd been asleep. Needing to say the words as well, she told him, "I promise, Daddy."

She heard his quick inhale as she called him that name. She crossed her fingers, hoping it would please him.

"You are so special to me, Caroline. I swear to be the best Daddy in the world."

"You don't have to be that, just be my best Daddy," she suggested.

"You've got it, Precious."

A thought crossed her mind. "Don't you have steaks outside?"

"I'm going to go put them on now. I saw you were in the nursery and wanted to explain."

"I understand, Daddy."

"Good girl. Go scope out the rest of the house. Maybe we can play in here after dinner."

"I'd love that."

He kissed her on the forehead before stepping away. When his footsteps faded on the thick carpet, Caroline forced herself to leave the adorable room for a few minutes to tour the rest of the cabin. The next doorway revealed a guest room with a desk and a computer. Maybe he'd let her type in here? Suddenly, she could see herself spending a lot of time in wooded seclusion.

Leaving that room on that positive thought, Caroline walked into the main bedroom. A massive bed stood in the middle. That had to be more than a king-size. The bedframe was heavy, dark wood with interesting metal decorations. She leaned over one side to see better and gasped. That wasn't an embellishment. It was an iron loop.

An image of being tied on Wraith's bed burst into her mind. She couldn't imagine the pleasure he could subject her to if he bound her completely at his mercy. She shivered in anticipation.

Would he allow her to tie him up? Maybe if she was very, very good.

Forcing herself to turn away from that delectable fantasy, Caroline checked out the rest of the room. It was quite a comfortable space. Masculine and homey, with its dark wood and tan walls. She had a sudden flash of a pile of pink pillows scattered at the top of the bed. Grinning at the combination of his style and hers, Caroline realized she could see their relationship lasting far into the future. She'd never envisioned that with Adam.

She wrapped her arms around herself in a giant hug. To her delight, Wraith appeared like magic to embrace her from behind. Caroline treasured the sensation of his powerful arms encircling her. She leaned against his hard torso and asked, "How do you feel about pink pillows?"

"My interior design sense is tingling with excitement," he answered drolly.

"I hoped you'd agree."

"Did you check out the attached bathroom?"

"Why, do you have exciting features, like a bidet toilet seat?" Caroline teased.

"Now that's on my to-buy list. Maybe if you're a good girl, I'll let you play with the jets."

A shiver of anticipation ran through her. She had picked up quickly that when his voice lowered, she needed to pay attention. Something yummy was coming. "What is it really?"

"Go look."

"Hey!" Caroline headed for the bathroom when he stepped back and popped her on the butt to jumpstart her. Wraith winked at her. That slow gesture did crazy things to her inside.

Damn, she'd missed him.

Walking into the bathroom, she noted a huge, clear shower. The image of seeing him through the steamy glass popped into her mind. Oh, yeah. Or it was big enough for two. Even better.

When she turned around, Caroline spotted the large soaking tub. "Four people could fit in that!"

"Only two will ever be in there. A Little girl needs a tub for bath time. I have some toys under the cabinet. Maybe you'd like a bath before bed?"

"I'm really dirty," she rushed to tell him before realizing what she'd implied. Her cheeks heated, and she slapped her hands over her face to hide in embarrassment.

"Yeah, I've figured that out," he growled.

Caroline peeked between her fingers to find him watching her closely. "Is that a good thing?" she whispered.

"The best. I need to get back to the grill or we'll eat charcoal for dinner. Do you want to come hang out with me on the porch or would you rather play in your nursery?" he asked.

"Can I stop and get that purple monkey in the nursery? Adam threw out all my stuffies to hurt me. I haven't been able to buy any more. I didn't want to be disloyal to my old friends. But he's already there, and maybe he needs some love?" she asked.

"He definitely does. And if I ever see that jerk ex-husband of yours at Inferno again, he won't like the new shape of his nose."

"He's not important, Wraith. You're bigger, stronger, and better for me."

"Still," Wraith grumbled as he turned to head for the front of the house. "Get your buddy and come sit on my lap. I need to hold you, Precious."

His butt flexed enticingly as he walked in front of her down the hall, making her almost forget to detour into the nursery to pick up her new friend. Caroline sat on the carpet in front of the crib where she'd spotted the monkey.

"Hi. I'm Caroline. Could we be friends?"

The monkey studied her with big, black eyes. He seemed to consider her request. Caroline sweetened the deal.

"I'll never let you get dusty, and I'll give you hugs and kisses."

I accept.

"You need a name. What do you think of Jam?"

A happy feeling filled her mind. Jam liked his name.

"I like it too. Want to sit on my Daddy's lap with me?"

I've been waiting for you to come. Please give me a hug now.

Caroline rose to her knees and scooped Jam up in her hands. She wrapped her arms around him and squeezed him so tight. They were instantly the best of friends.

"Come on Jam. Let's go hang with Daddy."

Feeling happier than she ever remembered being, Caroline skipped down the hall and out the back door. The setting sun had robbed the air of some of its warmth. She was glad to snuggle into Wraith's warmth as he enfolded her in his embrace. He fit around her as perfectly as she remembered. Exhaling a sigh of contentment, she laid her head on his shoulder.

"I've missed you so much," she whispered.

His arms tightened around her in a gentle squeeze. "The Devils were considering voting me out. According to them, I've been a complete jerk."

"I don't think they said jerk," she teased.

"You would be right. Introduce me to your new friend. Does he have a name?"

Feeling self conscious, Caroline showed him her stuffie. "This is Jam."

"That is a perfect name!" he praised her. "Hi, Jam."

After a pause, Wraith asked, "Why did you come now, Precious?"

"This is going to sound weird," she warned.

"When I'm holding you, I can handle just about anything."

"I never told you what I do for a living." Caroline sat up slightly so she could watch his reaction. So much hinged on this. Would he understand why she hadn't told him? "I'm an author. I write romance novels."

"Fun. Do you have some published?"

"Yes. I have five already out there. They do well with readers, but I haven't ever found my niche. The night we met, I was doing research for a new series."

"Okay. That's why you were on your phone so much. You were taking notes?"

"Exactly. Inferno seemed like a great place to get a handle on bikers." She remembered the type of handle she'd gotten on one particular biker and got flustered. "I mean, understand how they operate and see an MC in action."

His hand patted her bottom. "I understood that. So, how does that affect you deciding to come see me?"

"Yesterday, I finished my first MC romance. It forced me to focus on my feelings and figure out why I panicked. I cried so much as I wrote it. I poured my feelings into the book. It's probably my best work yet."

"Congratulations, Caroline." He celebrated with her before prompting her. "And when you finished?"

"I knew my connection to you was more than infatuation or excitement about having a bad boy in my life. You could be a sacker at the grocery store, and I'd be sure you're mine."

"So, you came to test out the attraction to see if it was real?"

She could hear the hesitation in his voice. "No. I came to beg you to give me a second chance. To see if we," she waved a hand back and forth between them, "could repair this."

Wraith sat quietly for several seconds. Caroline gave him time, dealing with the apprehension that built inside her with every moment that passed. "Thank you for explaining, Little girl. I'm proud of you. You were very brave."

"Why didn't you try to see me?"

"You were scared of me, Precious. If I'd appeared at your condo, how would you have reacted? With fear or with happiness?"

"I can't tell you that."

"That's why I didn't show up at your door. I better get those steaks before they're charcoal." Wraith scooped her up as he stood and placed Caroline gently on the warm chair. He opened a storage chest and pulled out a wrapped package. Ripping the packaging away, he draped the soft gray fabric over her before he left the screened-in porch.

Squirming into a comfortable position in the cushions Wraith had warmed, Caroline pulled the throw up to her chin and snuggled the blanket close. She smoothed a hand over the plush material. She loved how it felt on her skin. After rubbing a handful against her cheek, she tucked it under her chin.

"You look as comfortable as a bug in a rug," Wraith teased when he returned.

"I love this, Daddy."

"I'm glad. Lucien gifts each of the Devil Daddies a blanket to give to their Little girl. If you run your hand down to the corner, you'll find our logo printed there. It's his way of welcoming you to our family."

"You only get one? Do you want me to put this back in the bag?" she asked, realizing this was much more than a simple cover.

"It's yours now, Little girl. I've given it to you."

Incredibly touched, Caroline blinked away the moisture that

gathered in her eyes. What had she ever done to deserve this man? "Thank you, Wraith."

"You are very welcome. Now, I'm headed into the kitchen to grab a plate to pull the steaks off the grill. It's getting chilly out here. Bring your blankie and Jam, and we'll go inside."

"Can I set the table?"

"Yes, Precious. You can set the table for me."

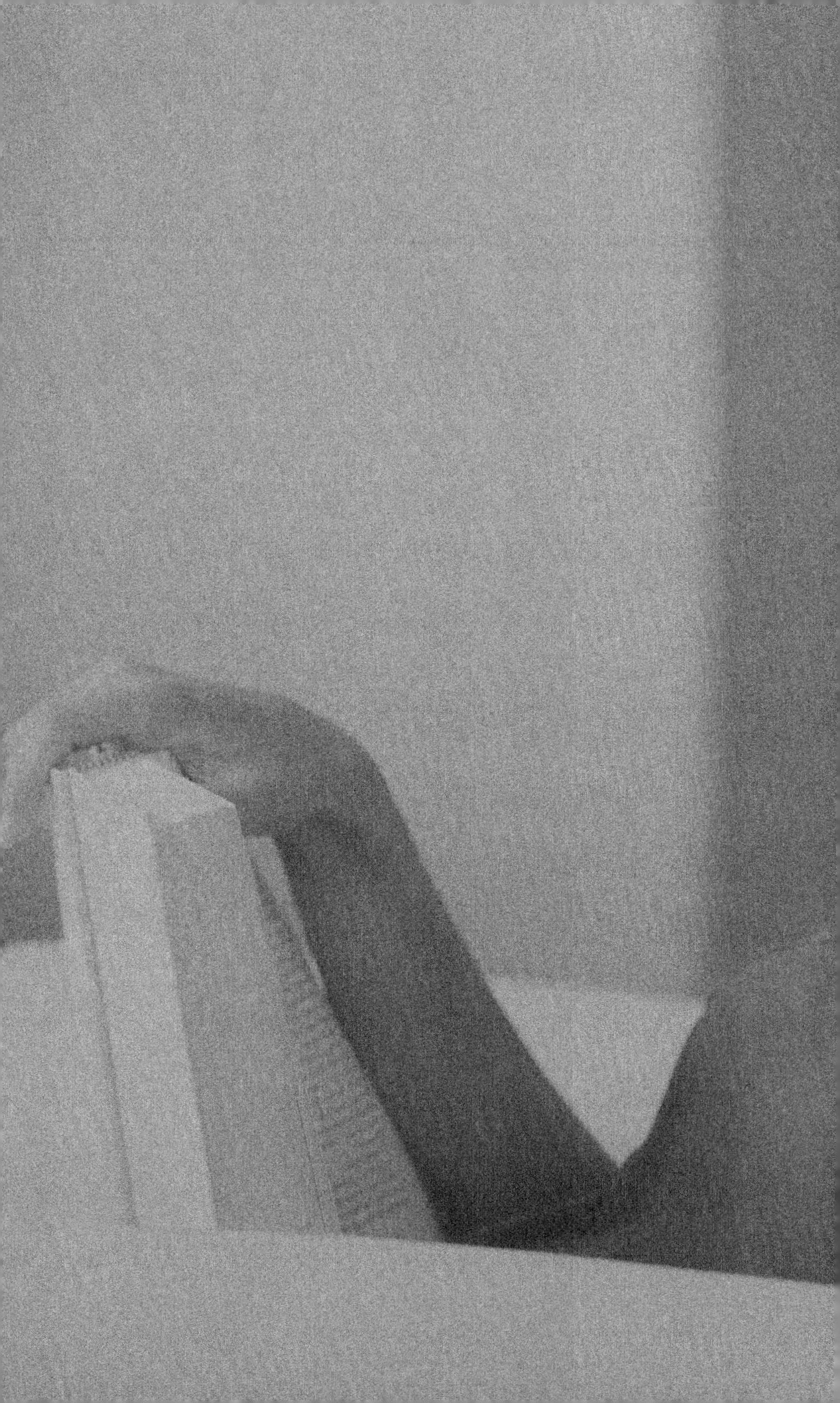

CHAPTER 9

Caroline put down her fork with a sigh of delight. "I'm so full. You're a phenomenal cook. That steak was perfect."

"Would you like more mac and cheese?" he asked, holding out a spoonful to drop on her plate.

"No way. I'm stuffed. You eat it." She grinned when he followed her suggestion and popped the serving spoon into his mouth to polish it off.

Dining with Wraith was completely low stress. He didn't care how much she ate, and judging from tonight, the amount he consumed would always exceed hers. In a world where guys often expected women to eat dainty portions, it was a relief to relax and consume what she wanted. Best of all, Wraith had included healthy additions on the dinner menu, so it wasn't like she was only dining on crap. She'd loaded up on salad and apple slices to balance out the more caloric steak and cheesy pasta.

"Mmm." He hummed with delight as he chewed.

"The dishes are mine," she announced, needing to do something to help.

"Not happening," he mumbled before swallowing. "Why

don't you and Jam choose a book on the shelf in the nursery, and we can read that after I finish putting this away?"

"That's not fair," she protested.

"My goal isn't to balance who does what around the house, Caroline. I want to take care of my Little girl."

How could she argue with that? She loved how he made her fantasies of having a Daddy come true. Caroline wanted to pinch herself to make sure she wasn't dreaming this. Wraith would frown on her hurting herself so she focused on his request. "Okay. Any preferences on the book?"

"Completely your choice. I picked out a bunch that sounded interesting. If you can't settle on one, try the close your eyes and point method." Wraith demonstrated by covering his eyes with a hand and moving his other back and forth in a row before pointing and grabbing that imaginary book.

"I'll go find one now," she said, pushing back from the table. After grabbing Jam and her blankie, Caroline dashed out of the kitchen.

She skidded to a slower pace when Wraith yelled, "No running in the house, Precious."

"Okay, Daddy."

Cuddling Jam close to her heart, Caroline kissed his head. "That's my Jam," she whispered and laughed at the joke she'd made, happy her monkey had liked that name too.

She turned on the lights in the nursery and headed for the shelves. Dropping to her knees, she carefully laid down her blankie before setting Jam on top and folding the soft material around him. The Devil Daddies logo looked perfect sitting on his tummy. A question popped into her mind to ask Wraith later.

"Daddy," Caroline corrected herself aloud and smiled. That sounded really good.

Scanning the spines on the shelf, she took her time considering each volume. Her gaze kept returning to one. That had to be the right choice. So she chose a book she hadn't heard of before based completely on a star at the top and a magic wand at the bottom. Caroline turned through a couple of pages and loved the illustrations scattered between sections of text.

"This is the one, Jam. I want to see what this is about."

She collected Jam, the blankie, and the book to take to the family room. Once there, she announced, "I hope you like this story!" The sight of Wraith's butt showcased in the kitchen as he leaned over the dishwasher made her mouth water. He glanced over his shoulder to catch her ogling him and lifted an eyebrow.

"Like what you see, Precious?"

"Mmmhmmm," she answered, nodding enthusiastically.

"I hope you chose a short story," he said, and she automatically understood he meant to ravish her as soon as they finished reading.

Sheepishly, she held up the thick book she had selected. "Oops?"

"I should let you digest your dinner before allowing you to do gymnastics."

A mental picture flashed into her head of making love with Wraith, and her cheeks heated with excitement.

"I'd love to peek into your brain to see what's going on in there, Little girl. I think we'll read a few chapters tonight and then have an early bedtime. Jam looks tired."

"Oh, he's exhausted," she assured him.

"Give me five more minutes, and I'll be right there. Curl up on the couch and talk to me."

"Okay, Daddy. What do you want to discuss?"

"Tell me about your writing," he suggested.

"I created my first book three years ago. It did well. Not gangbusters like making the New York Times Bestseller list, but I earn more money than I'd dreamed possible. Adam…."

"That asshole's name should never come out of your mouth again unless he's an imminent danger to you, Little girl."

Caroline swallowed hard at the animosity in his voice. "I'm sorry. There are things in my life that involve him. I didn't mean to upset you."

Wraith slammed a hand down on the counter and then apologized when she jumped. "Sorry, Caroline. I didn't mean to snap at you. I can't imagine someone being stupid enough to let you go. All I can think of is how much I want to tear off his balls and feed them to him for treating you poorly. That man is an idiot."

"He is," she said with a smile, loving how he sprang to her defense.

"I'll try not to react when I hear his name. I don't want to scare you."

"You didn't. You'd never hurt me."

"Your bottom is fair game," he said with a twinkle in his eye.

She squirmed on the couch as he stalked forward. "Maybe we could negotiate that?"

"Not happening. Keep going. Tell me what Adam, the idiot, said."

"You're going to refer to him like that every time now, aren't you?" Caroline asked, laughing. It was amazing how Wraith's protectiveness blunted the harm that Adam had done. Her ex-husband's power to affect her dwindled as Wraith showed her how a positive relationship could be.

"Yes." Wraith sat on the couch next to her and lifted Caroline onto his lap. "So, what did the idiot say?"

"He told me I was a one-hit wonder. And he was right. My second book didn't do as well. Still okay but didn't sell gangbusters. Same with the next stories. I switched categories of romance each time, searching for my groove. I think that was a terrible mistake. MC romance is super-hot right now. I loved writing my book. That might be the type of novel that will work for me."

"Are you going to stick with MC?"

"I am. It's fun to write, and I did a great job on it. We'll see what my editor says."

"I love a plan. That's not why you came back, right? So you'd have material or research for your book?" Wraith watched her closely.

"I'm glad you asked. I don't want that question repeating itself in your head." She shook her head before continuing. "No. I can do research online. You aren't my model for a bad biker dude. I wouldn't share you with anyone inside a book or out of one. You're all mine."

He stared at her for several seconds. Caroline's stomach flip-flopped inside her, and she clutched Jam a bit tighter. Please let him believe her.

Wraith wrapped his hand around the back of her head and drew Caroline's face close to his. "Thank you, Little girl, for explaining." He pressed his mouth to hers in a sweet kiss.

When he lifted his head, she closed the gap to plant a fiery smooch on his lips. Wraith responded immediately to her and swept his tongue into her mouth. She absolutely loved his taste—yummy dinner along with that flavor only Wraith had. He gave her butterflies in her tummy every time he was close.

When she sat back, he studied her for several long seconds before teasing, "Bad biker dude, huh?"

She waggled her eyebrows suggestively. "You're even better than that—bad, biker Daddy."

"I can live with that." He hugged her close before settling Caroline against his chest so his arms could wrap around her and hold the book. "Let's see what you chose."

Caroline leaned quickly to the side to pick up the book that had slid to the side during their distraction. "This one, Daddy. It looks good."

"I've heard great reviews about it. Let's see if we agree."

Wraith pointed to different things on the cover and asked questions before opening her selection. He thumbed slowly through the pages, checking out the illustrations on the endpapers lining the inside of the cover and reading the author note. By the time he got to chapter one, she could hardly wait.

His deep, gravelly voice wrapped around her, whisking Caroline away from reality and into the world of dragons, sorcerers, and magic. She'd forgotten how special it was to have someone read to her. Wraith created voices for the main characters and added drama in his tone to add tension and suspense as the action unrolled. She loved every minute.

"No! Read another chapter, Daddy," she protested as he marked their page with a piece of ribbon from the end table's drawer.

"Tomorrow night, Precious. I like this book. What do you think of it?"

"It's so good. That dragon is going to cause a lot of trouble. I'm afraid he's going to eat the princess! We should read another chapter to keep her safe," Caroline urged.

"I think I'm ready to channel my inner dragon," Wraith shared.

"You're going to eat a princess?" she asked. He gave her a single, knowing nod that made her review what she'd said. Her confusion evaporated. "Oh!"

"We'll read more tomorrow," he told her.

"Yes, Daddy."

"I like the sound of that. Come on, Little girl. I need to get the grill's smoke and the warehouse smell off me before we go to bed. Let's go tuck Jam into the covers and take a shower."

She scooted off his lap and waited for him to stand. Caroline was so flustered she forgot to pick up her stuffie and the blanket, but Wraith took care of both for her and tucked them under his arm. Holding her hand, he led the way to his bedroom.

"Settle Jam in bed and come into the bathroom. I'll go turn the water on to heat."

When he disappeared into the adjoining room, Caroline hurried to the far side of the bed. She guessed Wraith would want to sleep closest to the door. After placing Jam on her pillow, she stretched the blanket over him. Sure he would drift off in a minute, she eagerly walked into the bathroom.

Stopping in her tracks, Caroline spotted Wraith wearing nothing but his socks. He lifted one foot after another to strip those off before turning to face her. "One of us is seriously overdressed. Come here, Precious. Let me unwrap my package."

Too much time had passed since she'd gotten to see Wraith naked. She devoured his chiseled muscles with her eyes as she approached him. "Do you like lift cars to exercise?"

"No, Little girl. I work hard, but I also love the gym." He reached out to snag the hem of her shirt and lift it over her head as he continued to talk. "We have an extensive one here. I'd take you there, but you might decide to upgrade to someone else."

"I can't imagine that any of them are as ripped as you."

"Ripped, huh?"

Wraith tossed her shirt into the hamper before running his fingers along her throat to brush over the swell of her full breasts. When she gasped, he said, "Funny, I prefer soft and curvy."

Her heart beat faster as she celebrated his preferences. "I've got some curves," she suggested.

"So I see. I think I need to check out the rest." With a flick of his fingers, Wraith unfastened her bra and slid it from her body. He traced a line over her abdomen to her jeans and opened the fastener at the waistband before pulling the zipper down. He rubbed a small circle over her mound before sliding his hands inside her zipper, around her sides to cup her bottom. "Perfect curves."

He lowered her jeans to the floor as he squatted in front of her. "Put your hand on my shoulder to balance yourself, Little girl. Lift this foot." He tapped her toe. When she followed his directions, Wraith coached her through the other side. Her shoes, socks, and the heavy denim material flew toward the clothes hamper. Somehow, he tossed her sneakers next to it.

Her panties were next. She bit her bottom lip to hold back a moan of arousal as Wraith tugged those slowly down her legs. When he leaned forward to inhale her fragrance, slickness gushed from her to coat her inner thighs.

"Mmm," he hummed next to her skin, and the vibration spread through her mound.

"Wraith, please," she begged.

"I'm not rushing this, Precious. Step for Daddy," he coached and removed the scrap of lace. He rose to his feet, brushing her body with his before standing back and gripping her waist hard as he scanned her curves with a hungry look.

Caroline stood proudly as his gaze ran over her. She wouldn't allow any insecurities or self-doubt to sneak in when his expression told her how much he wanted her. He wrapped a powerful arm around her waist and hauled her to him to seize her mouth in a searing kiss. Eagerly, she rose to her tiptoes as she held on to his broad shoulders.

"I'm struggling to stay in control, Caroline. If you need me to ease up, tell me. Whenever. I'll rein myself in," he growled.

"I don't think I want you to do that, Wraith."

"Remember. I would hate to hurt you. Tell me if you're uncomfortable or need something else."

She nodded, understanding how close to the edge he was. His passion thrilled her that he was this into her, Caroline Sweets. "You can make love to me later, Wraith. Fuck me now."

He didn't hesitate. His arms tightened around her, hauling her toes from the floor. Wraith carried her into the shower stall, directly under the spray of warm water. He seemed to be everywhere as his hands roamed over her.

Living dangerously, Caroline nipped at his bottom lip, egging him on as she explored his hard frame. His response? Wraith tangled his fingers in her hair, yanking her head back to give him free access to her mouth and neck.

She shivered against him as her desire reached a feverish pitch. Stroking down his chest, she wrapped her fingers around his thick cock and squeezed. Wraith groaned and pulled her hands away.

"You're going to make me come before I can get buried inside you. Help me clean up so we can get out of here. My condoms are in the bedroom," he told her, his voice tense with sexual energy.

"I'm on birth control now, Wraith. It's safe. You can come inside me," she whispered, twirling her fingers over his bulky arms.

He stared at her hard for a second as he processed her words. Then, with a roar, he corralled her against the tile wall. She gasped at the feel of the chilly slate on her skin.

Bracing his hands on the surface behind her, he demanded, "Precious, tell me you're okay."

"The wall is cold. It will warm up, and I will be ecstatic as soon as you're inside me." Feeling sassy, Caroline winked.

"You're going to kill me, Little girl." He boosted her off the ground and demanded, "Wrap your legs around me."

As he settled against her, he brushed his fingertips down her torso to her plump mound. He explored her pink folds, teasing and tantalizing her as he ensured she was ready to take him. Her arousal soared higher as she realized how he put her needs first. When she writhed against the wall, he placed himself to her opening and pressed into her tight channel.

The stretch was absolutely delicious. Caroline tilted her chin up to concentrate on the sensations of Wraith, claiming every bit of space inside her. His shaft brushed over all the sensitive spots along its path, making her eyes roll back in her head with delight.

"Eyes on me, Little girl."

That steely demand brought her head up immediately. He locked gazes with her as he slid the last few challenging inches into her. "Damn, Caroline. You're wrapped around me like hot velvet. Nothing feels better."

"Move, Wraith. Push me over the edge. I need you."

"Hold on, Precious."

All the sensations swirled around her as he stroked in and out of her. One hand gripped her bottom tightly to support her as the other stroked over her curves. The warm spray of the water added extra stimulation as the steam wrapped around them.

Sliding her hands over Wraith's slippery flesh, she explored his strength. Caroline pressed her mouth to his corded neck and drew a line to his collarbone with the tip of her tongue. Savoring his salty, masculine flavor, she trailed kisses over his chest. To tease him, she licked his beaded nipple. Wraith's moan further clarified for her that his sensuality was boundless. Everything they enjoyed was acceptable, without limits. She smiled against his skin.

"You okay, Precious?" he asked.

"Better than okay. I missed you so much."

"Never again, Little girl."

His mouth took hers in a kiss that started hard and punishing before turning passionate and demanding. She tightened her legs around him and pulled Wraith's hips close, pressing him deeper. Wraith immediately responded, stroking in and out of her velvety channel with skillful plunges. He ground his pelvis to hers, demanding a response.

Her entire world shrank to the expanse of his shower. Forgetting everything else, Caroline could only focus on the sensations building inside her from her devastatingly skilled lover. Her first orgasm crashed over her without warning, making her cry out. The sound echoed on the hard surfaces and faded into oblivion as he drove her toward another.

Each round of pleasure blended into the next until she was forced to beg, "Wraith, come. I can't take any more."

"One more, Precious. Join me," he commanded as he increased the speed of his thrusts.

She nodded, wanting to please him. His hand, supporting her bottom, traced the cleft between her buttocks. Caroline had never played this intimately before. She held her breath as his finger drew close to her tightly clenched opening. Wraith wasn't dissuaded by her attempt to keep him out. He pressed that fingertip, slick with her juices, to that nerve-rich ring of muscles.

That was the last sensation she needed to orgasm. Caroline clamped around his thick shaft, and his cock swelled inside her and coated her walls with hot fluid. When his movements slowed, Wraith rested his head on her shoulder as he recovered his strength.

"So good," he whispered against her skin. It sounded like every ounce of his strength had evaporated.

"Let me down, Daddy."

Nodding, he eased her feet back to the ground. Caroline reached for his bodywash and smoothed it over his torso, removing the last vestiges of his day so he could rest.

"Thank you, Precious," he whispered as he ushered her out of the shower and dried their skin with soft, thirsty towels.

"Bed, Daddy." Linking her fingers with his, she led him from the bathroom.

He paused for a second to turn on a nightlight near the bathroom entrance. She stared at him. How did he know she had nightmares in the pitch dark?

"I guarantee the only monster in here that eats Little girls is me," he told her, making her giggle.

After a firm pat on her bottom, Wraith threw back the covers, taking care not to toss Jam from the bed, and urged Caroline into the crisp sheets before crawling in after her. He drew her close and pulled up the soft bedding before wrapping her in his arms and pressing a kiss on her forehead.

"Sweet dreams, Little girl."

"Sweet dreams, Daddy."

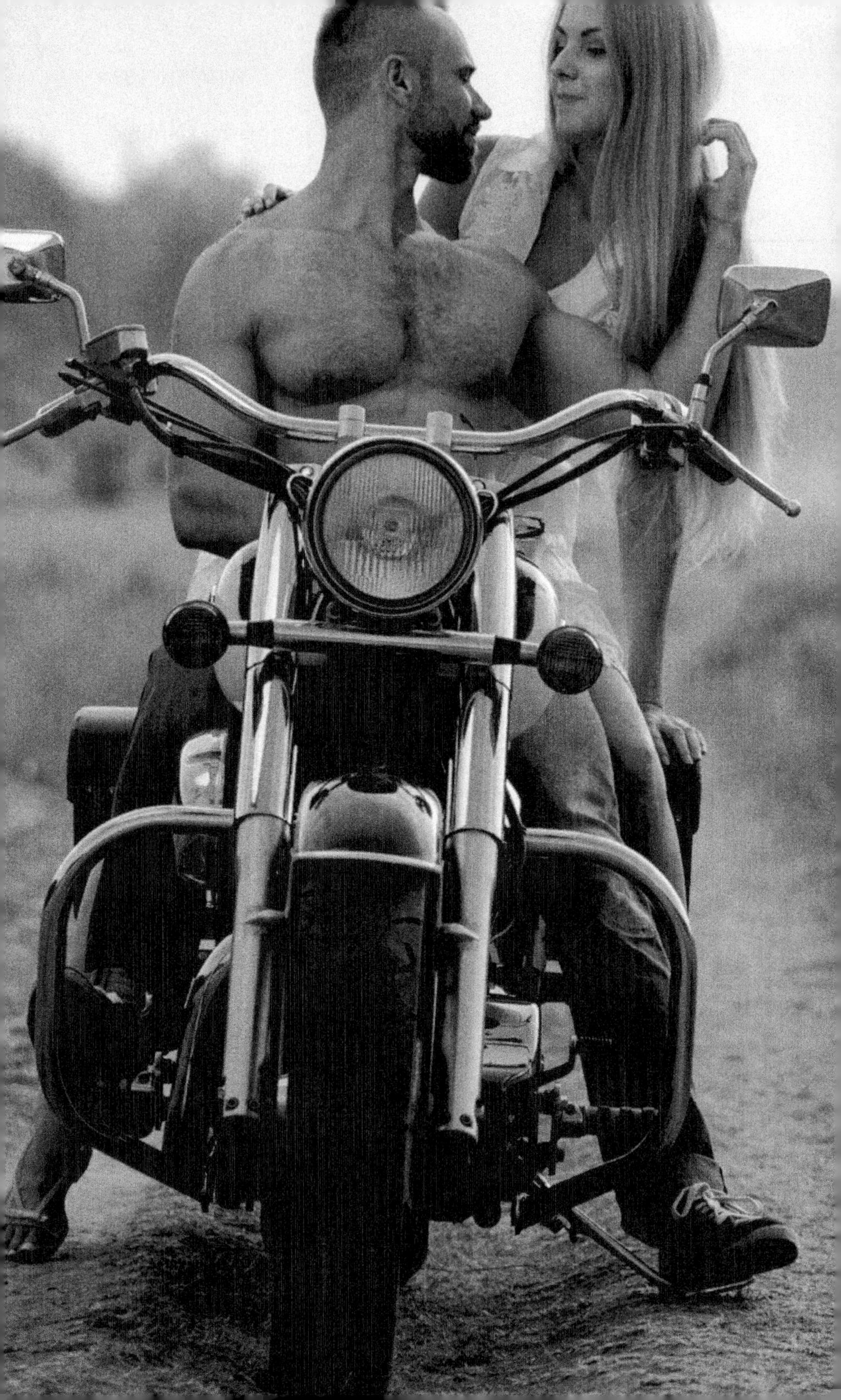

CHAPTER 10

Wraith's alarm sounded early the next morning. He kissed her before rolling out of bed. "Go back to sleep, Caroline. Call me when you wake up."

Closing her eyes in the dark room, she crashed into sleep. When she woke, the room was brightly lit. Caroline stared at the clock. 9:00 a.m.? That couldn't be right.

"Wraith?" she called, pushing herself up to sit in the middle of the spacious bed. No one answered.

Sliding out of bed, she opened a couple of drawers, searching for something to wear. When she found a T-shirt, Caroline pulled it over her head. Her first stop was the bathroom. Then she toured through the cabin, double-checking she was alone. On the kitchen counter sat a note.

Good morning, Caroline,
  It was difficult to leave you this morning. Give me a call.
  Daddy

• • •

He'd plugged her cellphone in for her a few inches away. Picking it up, she selected his number. He answered on the second ring.

"Precious."

She loved the warmth in his gravelly voice. "Hi, Daddy. I finally woke up."

"I zapped your energy, Little girl."

"Zapped. Is that what they call that?" she teased.

"It's become my favorite new term. There's breakfast for you in the refrigerator."

"You didn't have to do that," she protested, touched he had taken the time to do that for her in the early morning hours.

"Daddy's job. Eat and then relax. I won't be home too late."

"I'm going to head back to my apartment to write," she said quickly. She couldn't lounge around all day in his place while he worked.

"If you have to. I'd like you to pack some things and stay with me for a while. Bring your computer. You can create at my place. I like having you close."

"Like a couple of days?" she asked, trying to figure out what he had in mind.

"As long as you'll stay, Little girl. I'd like to have you with me."

"I'll go home and grab a few outfits. Can we talk about this when you're back?" she asked.

"I think that's a very good idea. They have your name at the gate to come and go as you like. I'll be back at the cabin around five, Caroline."

"I miss you, Daddy."

"You have no idea how hard it was to leave this morning, Precious. I'll be there as soon as possible."

She stared at the phone for a long time after she'd disconnected. Should she move in? Her apartment definitely didn't hold any appeal for her. This cabin seemed much more like home than her place ever had. It had simply been a shelter to live in when her marriage had crumbled.

Making her decision, Caroline set the phone down with a click. She opened the refrigerator to find scrambled eggs with bacon covered neatly by a sheet of plastic wrap. Suddenly ravenous, she popped the plate into the microwave. He took such good care of her.

After a long bath in the enormous tub, Caroline reclaimed her clothes from the laundry hamper. She didn't want to wear his T-shirt home with nothing else. Confiscating a pair of his stretch boxer briefs, Caroline giggled as she substituted those for her lacy panties. *Why is men's clothing more comfortable than women's?*

Returning to the bathroom, she noticed he had left a new toothbrush on the counter for her. How did she find this guy? She tore into the packaging and cleaned her teeth before storing the pink toothbrush next to his. The sight of them snuggled together in a glass made her heart happy.

Caroline snapped a quick photo and texted it to Wraith. His heart emoji answer fueled her dance back into the bedroom to grab her shoes and Jam. He had to come with her to pick up some things. He'd waited for her for too long. She wouldn't leave him behind.

She headed into the garage and opened the door using the wall-mounted control. After sliding into the driver's seat, she carefully backed out and paused to fasten her seatbelt.

"Crap! How am I going to close the door? I guess I can go in and out the front door," Caroline said to Jam. She noticed the purple monkey seemed to be focused on the glove box. Automatically, she followed his gaze. Remembering, she opened it to find the remote Wraith had given her last night. She took a second to attach it to her visor next to her condo's.

"Damn. He's good!"

After triggering the device, Caroline reversed carefully out of Wraith's driveway. Hitting a biker would be bad. She paused for a second to memorize his house number before heading out of the complex. A silver-fox biker she hadn't met before waved her out.

How many Devil Daddies were there in the MC?

Caroline dismissed the question from her mind as she concentrated on the secluded road toward Inferno. Emerging into the sunlight from the shaded tunnel of tree cover, she grabbed her sunglasses and popped them on. Inferno was quiet, with only a few bikes and cars in the parking lot as she drove through.

Once on the freeway, Caroline plotted what she needed to pack. She worried she would bring too much or too little, giving Wraith the wrong message, but then she remembered Wraith's words, "As long as you'll stay, Little girl. I'd like to have you with me."

She wanted to be with him. Caroline made a list of items to take care of while she was at her place. Empty the fridge, water the one plant she had…. Maybe she should bring that plant? Pack her large suitcase and her laptop.

With plans made, she organized everything quickly and piled things together. She made a trip to the dumpster with food that would spoil. Lifting her suitcase into her car was a challenge, but she made it. Caroline stood in her family room and looked around.

While this wasn't a permanent goodbye, she wouldn't miss this space. This condo had sheltered her when she'd been at her lowest points, following the end of her marriage and her panic about Wraith. It hadn't counted as home, but she would always appreciate having some place safe to hide from the world.

"And you wrote a new book here," she reminded herself aloud. Crafting a romance about people in love had challenged her as she recovered from her heartbreak over her failed union with Adam. Wraith had shown her that part of her wasn't dead.

Caroline had hope once again. She still expected that Adam would be a pain. Her life was ensnared with his. But he didn't have the same power over her that he had before Wraith. Plus, having a big, bad biker on her side would discourage him from being a complete ass.

A warm feeling filled her. She'd survived so much. Wraith made her believe her fantasies could come true. He gave Caroline back her hope and passion for life. Caroline wrapped her arms around herself and squeezed.

"Time to go, Jam. Let's go home to Wraith."

Pausing at the mail station to empty her box, Caroline noted she'd have to remember to pick up her mail from time to time. She'd enrolled her regular bills in automatic payments from her bank account, so she didn't have to stress too much. But random things could slip through. With her to-do list complete, Caroline drove toward Wraith's home.

When she saw Inferno coming into sight, her phone rang. Caroline answered it through her blue-tooth connection, "Hi, Wraith! I'm on my way back to your cabin."

"Stop and have lunch with me."

Would that gravelly voice ever stop being a turn-on?

"Are you there, Little girl?"

"Sorry, I had to concentrate on the road for a minute," she lied. "I'd love to spend time with you. Should I stop and pick something up?"

"I have lunch for you. I'll meet you at the back door of Inferno."

"I'm pulling into the parking lot. See you soon." Caroline loved that he wanted to see her so soon. She parked in her normal area and bounced up the steps at the entrance with her laptop bag thrown over her shoulder.

Spotting a biker at the door, she told him quickly, "I'm having lunch with...."

"Wraith. He alerted me, Caroline. I'm Fury."

"Hi, Fury. Nice to meet you."

"Don't keep him waiting," Fury said with a smile.

"Right. Thanks!"

When she turned the corner to see the back entrance, Caroline spotted Wraith's bulk. He immediately pushed away from the wall to stalk forward. She jogged forward to throw herself into his arms.

"I missed you, Little girl," he growled before bending her backward with a fiery kiss that made her forget they weren't alone.

When he lifted his head, she could only blink up at him.

"You going to work?" Wraith asked, taking the laptop bag that had somehow ended up in his hand and slinging it over his shoulder.

She'd totally forgotten. "Your kisses are dangerous," she whispered.

"I can live with that," he said with a smirk.

"I didn't want to leave it in the car, just in case. It has my world on it," she explained. When he raised an eyebrow, she amended that, "All my work world on it."

"A fool would break into a random car in the Inferno parking lot. A man with a need for pain would target the Little girl of a Devil Daddy."

She shook that thought from her mind. "I saved him a lot of trouble then, didn't I? Did you promise me lunch?"

"I did. Come on, Precious."

He took her hand and led her outside. A bunch of Devil Daddies MC members had gathered, hanging out behind the building. Feeling out of place, Caroline tucked herself behind his massive back. Wraith stopped and tugged her from hiding behind him. Caroline was thrilled she'd changed clothes and put on makeup before leaving her condo.

"This is Caroline. She's mine," Wraith explained.

They all nodded and stood to greet her. She could feel them studying her and knew they wouldn't forget her features. Wraith's claim on her made Caroline important to remember.

She recognized a few faces: Scythe, of course, Fury, and Lucien, the owner.

The latter stepped forward to consider her. Caroline didn't understand all his tattoos, but her biker research clued her in that some were vaguely prison-related. How dangerous was this man? Would he give her another chance after she'd fled from his MC brother? Wraith squeezed her hand to reassure her when her fingers tightened on his.

"Welcome, Caroline. The Devil Daddies MC recognizes you."

"Thank you, Lucien," Wraith said as Caroline wondered what that meant. Quickly, she collected herself to say something.

"Yes, thank you, Lucien. It's nice to meet you all."

"Such nice manners. You've chosen well, Wraith. Is she staying with you?"

"Yes."

"Good. Priceless treasures should be protected," Lucien stated and nodded to excuse himself as he returned to Inferno.

Caroline breathed a sigh of relief. His tone was free of censure. She'd wondered how Lucien would react to her after she'd run from his MC brother. He didn't look like someone who'd forgive or forget easily.

Wraith interrupted her whirling thoughts. "Let me introduce you to the others. You've met Scythe and Fury. I'll start on the right: Pirate, Street, and Toxin."

"Hi," she said with a wave. She'd never remember all those names. "I hope there's not a test."

"Never," Wraith reassured her before wrapping his arm around her and guiding her away. "Come on, Caroline. We'll have lunch over there."

Caroline followed him closely. The bikers were definitely different from the people she'd always hung out with, but they'd greeted her warmly. A thousand questions tumbled around in her mind, distracting her as they walked. When Wraith stopped suddenly, she ran smack into him.

"Uff! I'm sorry," she rushed to say.

"You're cute when you're nervous," Wraith complimented her.

"I've got a lot of questions. Can I ask them when we're at home?" She definitely didn't want to say anything wrong here.

"Of course. We can sit on this bench," Wraith told her, pointing to the secluded spot. He set her computer bag safely on the ground next to them and sat down.

As he pulled things out of a cooler, she couldn't help but notice that deep lines were carved into his face. "I'm sorry you didn't get enough sleep."

"I'm not. I only need about four hours and I'm fine. We had a snafu that caused a flurry of work this morning. It zapped my energy."

"I hope it is okay now."

"Everything is better when you're with me, Caroline," he told her softly. Wraith reached for her and drew her face to his. "So much better." He pressed his lips to hers in the sweetest kiss. It brought moisture to her eyes.

"You're going to make me cry," she whispered when he released her.

"No crying. We're happy to be together. Now, let me feed you. Ham and cheese or turkey?"

"Did you make this for yourself?" she asked in wonder.

"I threw in a sandwich for you if you could come join me."

Caroline scanned the pile of sandwiches on the cooler and looked at Wraith's physique. It probably required a lot of food to power that strength. "I'll take turkey."

"You got it. How did things go in your condo?"

"I barely got my suitcase in my car. You're going to think I'm moving in," she warned, watching his reaction. Was this really what he wanted?

"Moving in is great. I wish I could have helped. I'll go with you for the next load," he promised.

"We're not going too fast for you?"

"No. How do you feel about it?" he asked.

"Good. It makes me happy to be with you," she told him honestly.

His smile transformed his face. "Having you close is important to me as well, Little girl. Did Jam go with you?"

"He's snuggling with my computer," she admitted.

"Eat, Caroline," he encouraged.

Their conversation for the next twenty minutes was light and fun. She loved hanging out with him. Caroline noticed the guys leaving from their gathering place. He'd have to return to work. "I'll see you at the cabin later?"

"I'll be there around five thirty."

"Do you need to work at Inferno?"

"Not tonight. Pirate is filling my place to give us time alone. Leave that suitcase in your car and I'll pull it out when I get home."

"Thanks. I'll go back and write this afternoon. I feel pretty inspired."

His eyes darkened with desire at her reference to their previous evening's activities. "I'll enjoy sparking new ideas for your books."

"Find Razor!"

That cry made them both whirl around. Wraith leapt to his feet and was off in a flash. He ripped open the door to Inferno and raced inside.

Caroline's heart pounded. What was going on? Wraith hadn't asked any questions but had reacted instantly. Feeling powerless to help what had to be an urgent situation, Caroline busied herself with gathering the remains of their lunch and packing everything back in his cooler.

She hadn't finished when Wraith returned with a man with silver hair who carried a satchel. Was that a doctor's bag? As they reached the concrete pad outside Inferno, four bikers appeared, carrying someone.

"Set him down," the man with the bag directed firmly.

That must be Razor.

He was handsome with silvery black hair. His serious expression wasn't panicked. Caroline immediately felt he was in control of the situation. Even in the scary situation, that reassured her.

Everyone complied instantly, gently placing him down on the solid surface. Razor dropped to a knee next to him and barked orders. Blood was everywhere, making Caroline queasy. Had that guy been shot? Why would someone do that? The Devil Daddies didn't waste time on speculation. They were completely focused on their MC brother.

"Give me your belt," Razor said, making eye contact with one biker.

Caroline stood a distance away, but she could tell he'd been dangerously wounded by the blood that spilled onto the cement. She brought her hands to her heart. Unable to see his face, she worried for whoever that was. Should she call an ambulance?

As that thought crossed her mind, the wail of a siren sounded and grew louder. Blood coated Razor's hands as he worked to staunch the wounds. With the leather strip tightened around the injured man's thigh as a tourniquet, he called for material to use for pressure bandages. All the men ripped off their shirts without hesitating.

"Wraith, I need pressure on this spot, too. Put those muscles to use. Push hard here."

Wraith had instantly lowered himself to the man's side. He followed Razor's directions and squashed the fabric tightly to the man's abdomen. By the time the ambulance rolled up through the warehouse's entrance, Razor had him stabilized. He quickly joined the emergency medical technicians in the ambulance as they rushed the injured man to the hospital.

"What the fuck happened?" Lucien demanded as soon as the doors closed.

"I don't know, Boss. Hellcat pulled in like that. There are bullet holes in the truck. The load is secure," a biker answered. Caroline thought he was Toxin.

"Bullet wounds will have the police here to investigate. Pull the cargo off and stash it where they can't find it," Lucien said. "Grab everyone to help."

Wraith ran to her side with hands stained with blood. "Go back to the cabin. I'll be there when I can."

He didn't stay for her to answer but raced off after the others. Caroline started for the door and remembered her laptop. She returned to the bench to grab it.

As she debated whether she should grab Wraith's cooler, Lucien said her name from behind. She whirled to face him.

"Go to the cabin. Wraith will take care of it."

She nodded and slung her bag over her shoulder. Turning, she walked toward the door.

"Caroline."

When she spun to face Lucien, he added, "Not everything is as it appears. Trust Wraith."

"Okay," she whispered and dashed for the door.

A few minutes later, she sat in her car and tried to figure out what had happened. A man had gotten shot and horribly wounded. Razor had identified himself as a doctor to the EMTs. Even she had noticed his skill as he worked to save the man's life. Then Lucien had sent everyone to hide the cargo. What was going on?

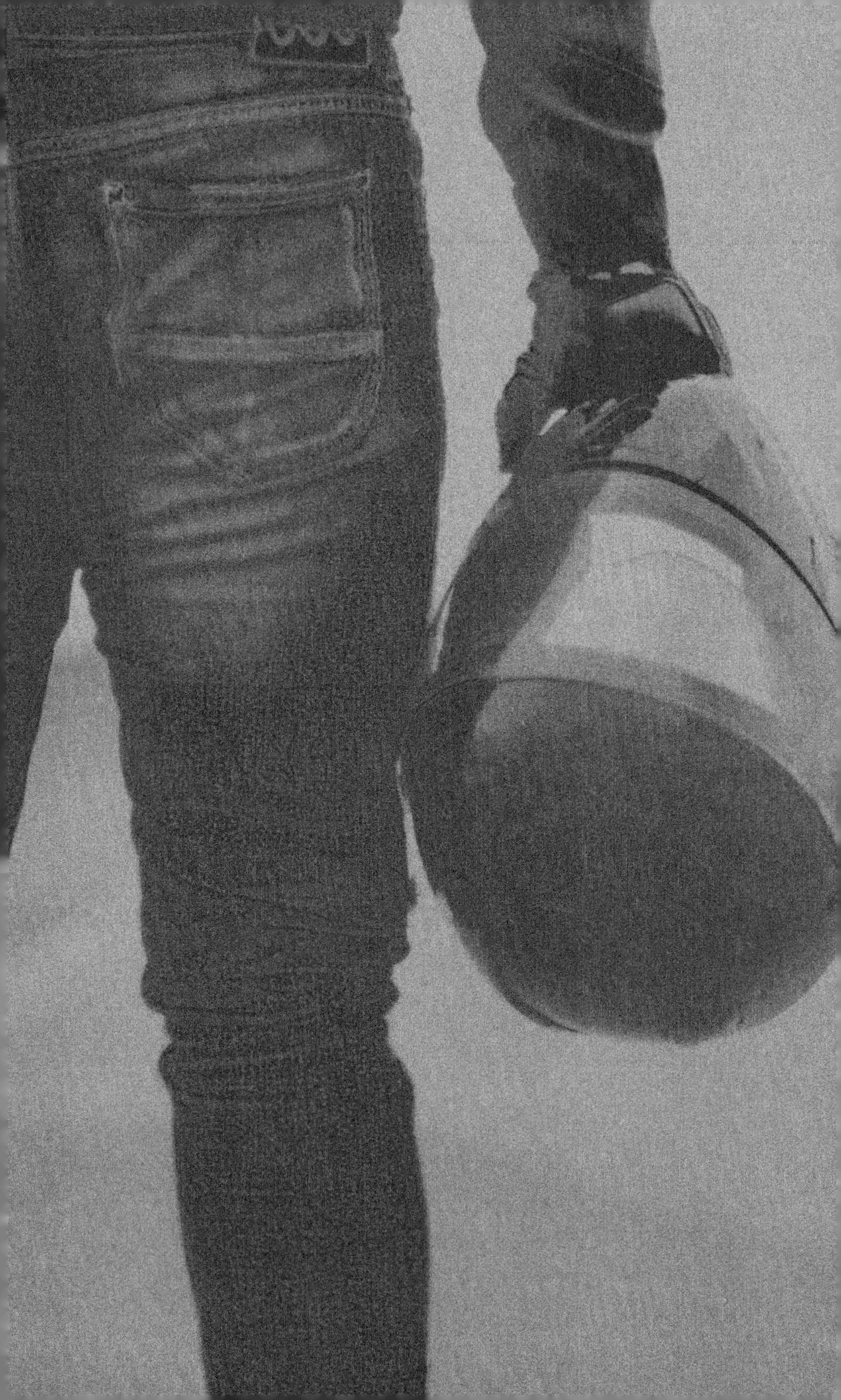

CHAPTER 11

Wraith stepped off his bike, and the last dregs of his energy evaporated. As he removed his helmet, he struggled to pull himself together to present a better image for Caroline. She'd have a lot of questions. With a shake of his head, he grabbed his cooler from its spot, secured on his rear rack by bungie cords, to go inside.

Turning around, he headed for the kitchen entrance from the garage and stopped in his tracks. Caroline sat quietly on the step with her arms wrapped around her shins. "Hi, Precious."

"Hi, Daddy. Are you okay?"

"I am. I bet you got scared today." He didn't tell her he'd called the front gate several times to see if she'd left.

She nodded. "I bet you can't share with me what happened."

"Not everything. I can tell you that Hellcat made it through surgery with flying colors. He's going to be fine in a couple of days."

"I'm glad. Are you okay?"

"Tired. But glad to come home to you. I was afraid you'd leave."

"I won't do that," Caroline promised.

The tension that had built inside him all afternoon unraveled.

Caroline hadn't run. Despite the frightening incident, she'd hung around. "Thank you, Little girl. Let's go inside, and I'll make us some dinner." He held out a hand for hers and tugged Caroline to her feet. Wrapping his arm around her, he pressed a kiss to her forehead before opening the door.

The aroma of Italian spices, tomato, and cheese filled his senses. Wraith's stomach growled loudly. "That smells amazing. Did you cook?"

"I got pizza delivered to the front gate."

"Romanelli's?" he asked, inhaling deeply. "I saw Pirate at the gate inhaling a pizza."

"I got an extra one for whoever was on duty. Smelling Romanelli's without a pizza to eat is torture I wouldn't wish on anyone."

"You've made a buddy for life. No wonder Pirate greeted me with a smile. That guy's never happy. I don't scare easily, but that grin gave me the willies," Wraith admitted, loving her grin in response.

"He is very serious. Pirate couldn't believe I brought him a paper plate, napkins, and some plasticware for his meal," she told Wraith.

A bark of laughter erupted from him at the thought of Pirate dabbing his mouth with a napkin and eating with a plastic fork. "Some men have no manners." He set the cooler down on the table and pulled her close. "Guess what I need more than half of that pizza in my belly."

Clueless, Caroline stared up at him in concern before slowly shaking her head and shrugging.

"Twelve kisses."

"Why twelve?" she asked in confusion.

"Because I'm a greedy bastard who really wants twenty, but I'm also so hungry I could eat that cardboard box. It seemed like a reasonable number to tide me over until after dinner."

"You!" she said, swatting playfully at his chest. Caroline rose onto her tiptoes to press her lips to his.

To Wraith's delight, she didn't start with a sweet, light smooch. His Little girl seemed to realize what he needed. She demanded his attention and got it. On kiss number ten, she dropped to her heels.

"Wait. I get two more," he reminded her.

"Not until you eat something. I can feel you getting emaciated." She patted his hard abdomen.

"I'll let you win this one, Precious."

"Thank you, Daddy."

Wraith put two large pieces on a plate she'd already set out and handed it to her. "Go sit at the table." After grabbing a slice for himself and taking a huge bite, he grabbed the pizza box from the counter and carried it with him. When she hesitated to choose a chair, he put the box on the table before pulling out one next to his normal spot. He waited for her to sit before sliding the chair into place. Munching on the slice in his hand, Wraith selected two bottles of water from the fridge and brought them to the table.

He popped the last bite into his mouth and opened her bottle as he joined her. "Drink. I'm willing to bet you haven't had enough water today."

She rolled her eyes at him but followed his directions. Yep, he was right.

Wraith helped himself to a second piece of pizza and inhaled it as fast as the first. "This is superb, Little girl. Thank you for ordering for us. I owe you some money. I'll leave a credit card in the box on the coffee table. You can use it in the future."

Her gaze changed from friendly to pointed—like with a sharp knife. "I'm glad to pay for things too, Wraith. I make a good income."

"Of course you do, Caroline. I wasn't insinuating you need my money. I enjoy taking care of you," he said softly.

When her posture softened, he hooked the toe of his boot around the leg of her chair and pulled her close. When she was in arm's range, he scooped her onto his lap. "Daddies stumble into dangerous territory sometimes. Now I understand that you're touchy about finances. Forgive me?"

She stared him down for a second before sighing. "Sorry. Adam always belittled the money I brought in. Even when I did very well."

"I'm definitely not Adam," he reminded her, curbing his tone to soften his anger at her ex-husband. "Tell me what else that bastard did that I need to avoid."

"I'd appreciate it if you'd not have an affair with a coworker."

"Razor was spectacularly heroic today, but I think I can refrain from having a fling with him."

When she laughed, he relaxed. He'd negotiated through that danger zone. Feeling he needed to be completely transparent, Wraith added, "There are some MC brothers who are bi or gay, but the Devil Daddies are all Doms. I don't make a good sub."

She shook her head at that idea. "And all the hotties at Inferno?"

"I could have chosen one of them before I met you. I didn't because they weren't my Little girl. Jeopardizing this," he waved a hand back and forth between them, "won't happen."

"I'm being ridiculous, aren't I?" she asked, feeling sheepish.

"Not at all. It's better to get everything out in the open than let negative thoughts fester."

"Are you a criminal?" she blurted.

"Have I done things against the law?" he asked. When she nodded, Wraith told her, "For the right reason, yes. Would I make the same choices again? Yes. Can you be okay with that?"

"I'm not sure," she answered.

"Then I'll try to reassure you, and we'll take some time for you to decide. Now, drink and eat. Romanelli's needs to be eaten fresh."

"Yes, Daddy."

"Having lunch with you was the highlight of my day. We'll have to make that a regular habit."

"Do the other Devils think I'm weird?" Caroline asked.

"No. Do you think they're weird?" Wraith reversed the question, attempting to get a handle on why she'd thought it was important to ask that.

"No, of course not. I guess for them, being a Daddy is something they've understood about themselves for a while."

"And you weren't aware you were Little?" he probed.

"I didn't even know Littles existed. I dated a bit in high school and college—nothing serious until Adam. Everyone was normal."

"Or they pretended to be normal," he suggested. Wraith noted she'd married the jerk who'd pursued her purposefully. What was up with his own sex who wanted size two women? Her next words drew Wraith from his thoughts.

"Possibly. I was pretty naïve and inexperienced. The last few years, a lot of eye-opening books released. I always have escaped into stories. Maybe that's why I love writing them."

"One of those novels you discovered was about Littles? Or age play?"

Caroline took a huge bite, making him suspect she wanted to give herself time to answer. Wraith didn't let her off the hook. He waited.

"Yes. The first one I read was about a young woman who applied for a job at a doctor's house. She didn't realize he was a Daddy, searching for a Little."

"That one sent you down a rabbit hole, huh?"

She nodded. "Something clicked inside me. I searched for as many of those books to understand more about myself. But I thought it was fiction—a fantasy. That people couldn't actually live like that."

"But they can. We'll explore and see what you enjoy and what doesn't do it for you," Wraith suggested.

"And what you don't like?" Caroline added hesitantly.

"I love a lot of things, Little girl, but yes. I promise I'll be honest. Can you do the same?"

She nodded immediately. Caroline looked up at him with such trust that his heart swelled in his chest. Wraith was in awe of their connection. Caroline didn't understand how special it was, but he did.

"Thank you, Little girl. Would you like another piece of pizza?"

"No, thank you. You eat that last one, Daddy. Then maybe you'd read more of the story?"

"You have very good ideas, Little girl."

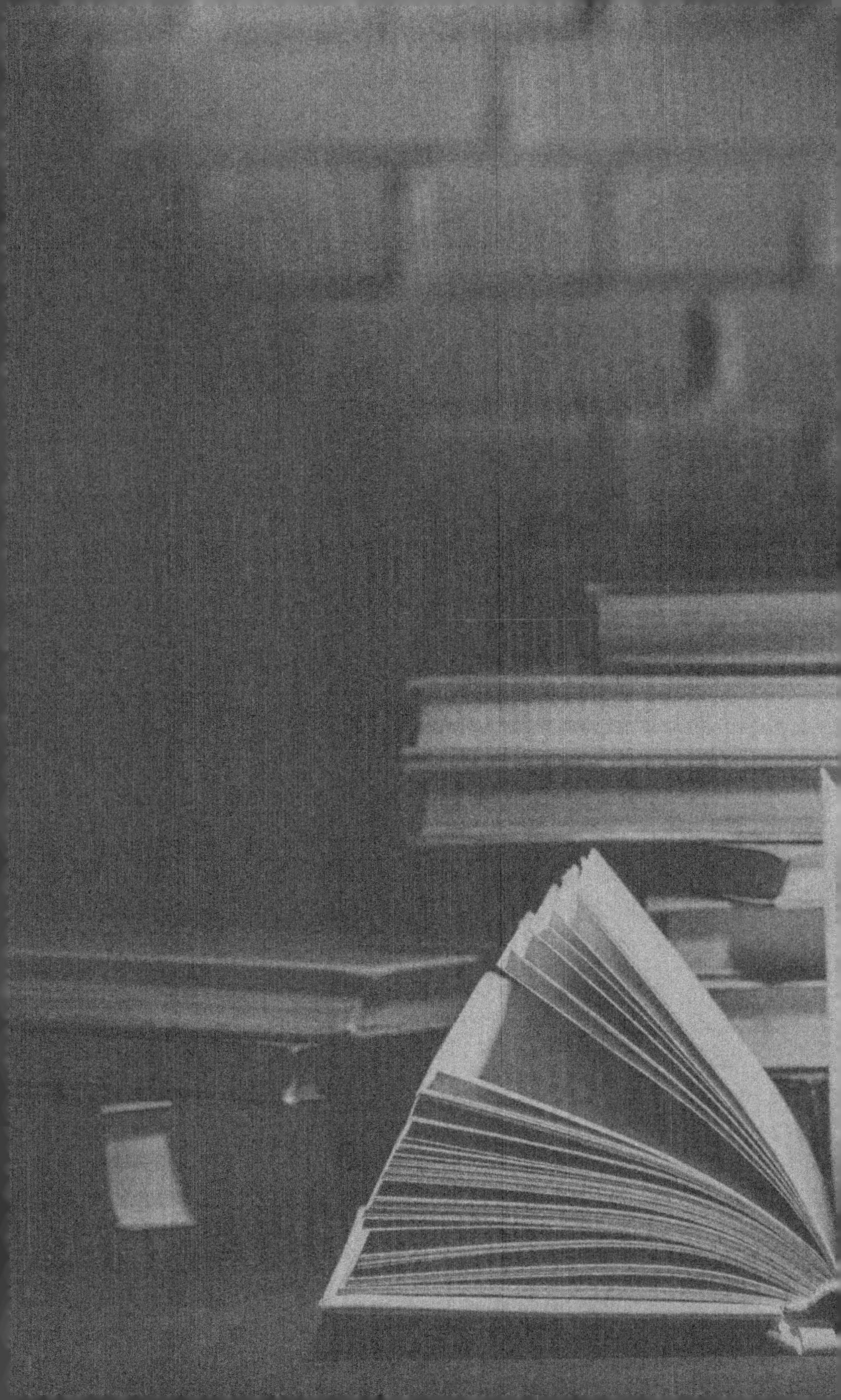

CHAPTER 12

A mustache tickling her most private area woke Caroline up in the middle of the night. Her legs draped over his shoulders as Wraith nibbled and licked her pussy. *He's so good at that!*

She reached between her legs to run her hands over his head, threading her fingers through his hair. Suddenly hot, Caroline threw back the rest of the covers that remained draped over her after Wraith's thick body had pushed most to the bottom of the bed. Propping her head up on one arm, Caroline peered through the darkness illuminated by the nightlight, and her juices gushed in response to the erotic view in front of her.

"Daddy," she whispered.

As if to reward her for using that name, Wraith slid two fingers into her tight channel so slowly she wondered if she'd lose her mind. His mouth continued to taste and tantalize her. When his lips closed around her clit and sucked firmly, those warning tingles she'd woken up to fused together into a climax that shook her.

Her fingers tightened in Wraith's hair, pulling him away from his snack. "You're killing me," she whispered, not complaining at all.

A slow smile spread Wraith's glistening wet lips. He pressed a kiss to her tummy as he crawled over her. Caroline loved how she felt caged underneath his bulk—protected and guarded. His thighs widened hers as he shifted upward, controlling her movements easily. His dominance thrilled her.

Wraith's mouth captured hers, feeding her intimate taste back to her. The thrill of savoring her own desire fueled urgent kisses as she wrapped her arms around his neck, clinging to his strength and power. She moaned against his lips when Wraith lowered his hips to thrust himself along her pink folds. Not entering her but rekindling the sizzling sensations she treasured.

He slid an arm under her waist and turned, reversing their position. Her pussy settled on his hard shaft, nestled close. Wraith spanned her waist with his huge hands and urged her up to sit, straddling his cock.

"Wraith! I don't like being on top," she whispered, feeling exposed.

"Let me change your mind. Give me five minutes." When she nodded, he brushed his hands over her torso to cup Caroline's full breasts. She moaned as he squeezed them firmly to distract her from her embarrassment.

"You are beautiful, Little girl. This may become my favorite position."

She could tell he wasn't lying. His expression was hungry, and his shaft jerked against her. Caroline shifted over him, deliberately sliding herself along his length. His fingers tightened, pulling a gasp from her as the heat flared hotter inside her. She liked the hint of pain.

"Put me inside you, Precious." Wraith released his hold to expand his caresses over her skin.

Caroline stroked her fingers down his muscular abdomen to wrap her fingers around his thickness. She rose onto her knees and rubbed the wide head against her, circling her entrance before fitting it in place. Descending slowly, Caroline dropped her head back as he filled her.

When her body finally rested on his, Wraith curled up to kiss her neck and shoulders. "You feel so good wrapped around me, Caroline. Can you stay here for me, Precious?"

Caroline nodded eagerly.

"Then I need you to move."

His hands wrapped around her hips as he settled back onto the mattress. His gaze devoured her. When she bounced tentatively, Wraith met her with a roll of his hips, grinding his thick root against her clit. She steadied herself, holding on to his thick forearms as he sent a thrill through her.

Hoping to please him, Caroline tightened her muscles around him and loved the groan that fell from his lips. She repeated the action as he continued his sweet torture. Soon, the self-consciousness faded from her brain. She could only focus on the gathering pleasure inside her and pushing his arousal higher.

"Come now, Little girl," he ordered as his thrusts up into her quickened with urgency.

Bouncing over him, Caroline screamed as the motion triggered an orgasm. Her channel clamped around on him, launching his climax as well. Hot fluid coated her inner walls, drawing a smaller pleasurable reaction. Wraith rose and gathered her into his arms, guiding Caroline down to his chest as their bodies pulsed together.

"Go back to sleep, Little girl."

Still fused as one, she closed her eyes and tumbled into sleep.

Caroline reached for Wraith's warmth and found only cool sheets. As she blinked her eyes open, she already sensed he was gone. She spotted Jam curled up on her Daddy's pillow and pulled him close as she checked the clock.

"No wonder the sheets were cold. He left hours ago."

How such a large man could move so quietly astounded her. Of course, he had worn her out in the middle of the night. Caroline smiled at that sizzling memory. Wraith must be a ninja with sex magic. She squeezed her legs together as the arousing fantasy of Wraith ravishing her in disguising clothes and a mask popped into her mind.

"Goodness. I have it bad," she told Jam. He'd understand her attraction to her Daddy.

When the purple monkey stared at her with knowing eyes, Caroline chose to get motivated. She slid out of bed and spread the covers up into place. With the task complete, she jumped in the shower to wake herself up.

With a cup of most writers' favorite fuel in her hand, Caroline wandered into the spare bedroom to reread what she'd written yesterday and see what she'd come up with today. Taking a sip of the coffee, she started her computer and checked her email. Unfortunately, she found an email from Adam. She clicked to open it and scanned the message.

It was ugly. She barely stopped herself from trashing it. Keeping it was wiser. Slumping in her chair, she read it again.

So your true colors have really come out now. Whoring yourself with an entire motorcycle club? That's lower than I would have expected. After I spent the night outside your condo waiting for you to come home, it's obvious you had other men to deal with. I'm attaching a letter from my lawyer. I'm taking you back to court for a higher percentage of your royalties. You owe me for keeping a roof over your head while you wrote that trash.

Adam

Horrified by his language toward her, Caroline clicked the attachment and read the legalese. Adam's fancy lawyer advertised he was a bulldog for men who faced nasty divorces. Her attorney had rolled her sleeves up and defended Caroline's interests while simultaneously rolling her eyes at his antics. Caroline would have to contact her. And pay the money to stop this move in its tracks.

No one had ever clued her in that books produced while you had a husband were considered marital assets. As the spouse of an author, Adam had a right to some of the money she earned on anything she'd written while they were together. This would never end if she didn't shut him down now. He'd come back year after year, wanting more.

After fortifying herself with another sip, she searched through her contacts and pulled up her lawyer's number.

"Dunworthy Esquire. How may I help you?"

The legal secretary's crisp voice made her smile. "Hi, Elizabeth. It's Caroline Sweets."

"Hi, Caroline. I'm glad to hear your voice, but I'm guessing this is bad news."

"Yes. I got an email from my ex-husband stating he was taking me to court for a higher percentage of my royalties. Could I make an appointment with Teresa?" she asked, naming her attorney.

"Of course. She has an opening this afternoon. A client canceled. Do you want to come in at two?"

"Yes, please, Elizabeth."

"I've added you to Teresa's schedule. Forward that email over to her with your ex's lawyer's name so she can prepare."

"On it. Thank you for your help."

Caroline dropped her head into her hands after disconnecting. Why did he have to be such a jerk? Her lawyer had recommended delaying the publication of any additional books for a year after the divorce. That way, Adam couldn't claim she'd written them while married to him. Without new books generating income, Caroline had worried about having enough money to cover her rent and expenses. If Adam got more of her dwindling earnings now, she'd have to skimp on everything to pay her bills.

Worst of all, she risked losing readers who would turn to another author while she had to wait so long to produce another book. Caroline crossed her fingers. *Please don't forget about me.*

Suddenly, writing held no appeal. She closed her laptop with a snap and walked out of her makeshift office. Pacing across the family room carpet, she seethed with anger. How dare he! Adam must be trying to impress another floozy and wanted her money to do it.

She should hire a private investigator. A real sleuth who could document all the crap he did. How did anyone go about finding someone to stalk a lowlife and get proof he was a complete jerk?

Caroline ran back to the office to grab her phone. The second her hand picked up the device, it rang. Without thinking, she tossed it into the air like it was a scorpion about to kill her. "Ahh!" As her scream echoed in the small space, Caroline tried to catch her tumbling phone. To her relief, it landed on the leather couch.

"Caroline? Is something wrong?" Wraith's deep voice sounded concerned. Somehow, she'd accepted the call when it rang.

"I dropped the phone. Hold on!" she called as she grabbed the device and unlocked it. When she had it securely in her hands, she pressed the speaker button. "It's okay. I've got it."

"What's going on, Precious?"

"You don't have time for this, Wraith, and it definitely isn't your problem. I'll handle it."

"You have two seconds to start talking or I'm headed home to spank your bottom beet red."

That wasn't a good visual image. She blabbed. "I got a message from Adam, my ex. He's going back to court to grab a higher percentage of my royalties."

"A higher percentage?" Wraith asked.

"Yes. He has rights to anything that I wrote while we were married."

"That's bullshit."

"It is. Now he's greedy and wants more. I'm sure he's trying to impress some twenty-year-old."

"Give me his address."

"I've already called my lawyer, Wraith. I have a meeting with her at two. Hopefully, she can shut this down. You don't have a private investigator in the Devils, do you?"

"I do. Tell me Adam's address and I'll have him checked out."

Caroline sagged with relief. "Oh, thank goodness. You're a lifesaver, Wraith. I'll text it to you." She sent him a message with that information. "You should have it now."

"Yep. Got it. I'll get someone on this," Wraith promised. "I probably won't have any information before your meeting at two. What's your lawyer's name? I'll make sure the details get to her as well."

"You are a prince among Daddies. Thank you, Wraith."

"I've got you, Little girl. Go write a sexy scene to read to me tonight."

"Wraith! I can't do that!"

"Of course you can. I can always use inspiration. I called to invite you to Inferno this evening. Would you come hang out with me while I man the front door? Come after your meeting, and I'll feed you some dinner before the crowd rolls in," he said.

"I'll see you in a few hours."

"Inspiration, Little girl. I want you to tell me about that chapter you're going to create. Go get busy."

"Yes, Sir. Daddy, Sir."

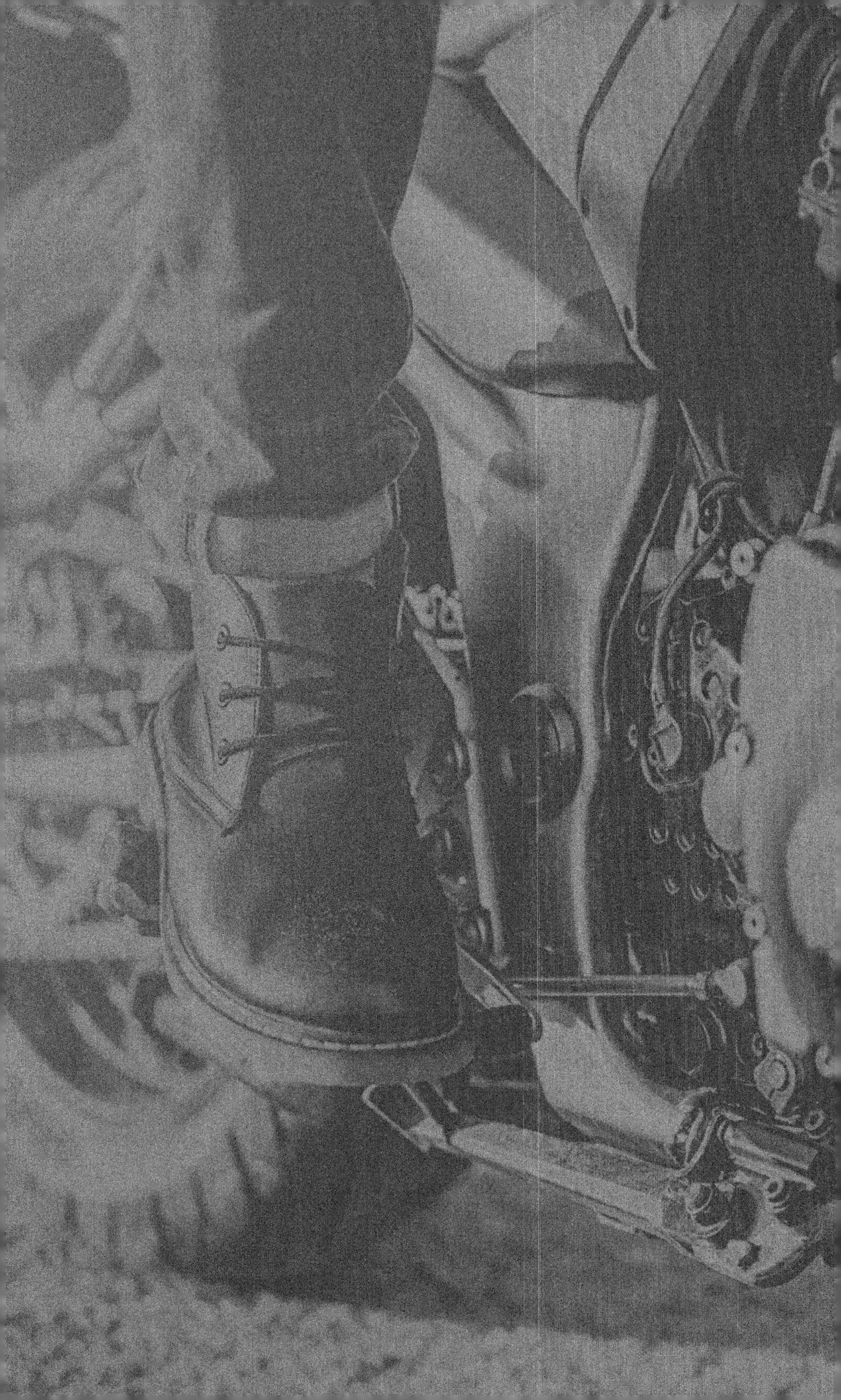

CHAPTER 13

"Lucien?" Wraith called his boss's name from the office doorway.

"Wraith. Come in. Is something wrong?"

"No. Everything is fine. The cops have finished their investigation. They're chalking the attack up to a random shooter by the highway. Throwing those shell casings into the truck and cab was smart. Thank goodness Fury thought to dig them out of the pallets as we unloaded the goods."

"Perfect. Is there anything I can do for you?" Lucien pushed his chair away from his desk and waved a hand toward the chairs facing him.

"Could you dig into a guy for me? He's my Little's ex. I need some dirt on him."

"Financial or women?"

"Either or both. He's going to sue Caroline for more money," Wraith told him.

"He's getting money from her?" Lucien asked.

"Yes. Legally, he's entitled to part of the royalties from her books."

"What kind of books?"

"Romance."

"Hmmm. That's interesting. She's not fucking you for research, is she?" Wraith bristled, and Lucien put his hands up. "Just checking. I'm sure you're being careful."

Lucien turned to his computer. "What's his name?"

"Adam McConnell."

"Address?"

Wraith recited it for him. He moved forward as Lucien typed quickly on his computer.

"Might as well come back here. You're going to want to read this." Lucien waved him around the desk and pointed at his screen. "This is his bank statement."

"I wonder what he blew five grand on. He almost emptied his account." Wraith focused on the bank's abbreviation for the vendor who'd collected that money. Anger boiled inside him. His Little girl was worried about money and her ex was tossing money around. He forced himself to focus on the details. "I can't tell where he spent that. Any ideas?"

"I do, but let's test my thought." Lucien copied the bank abbreviation and googled it.

A men's club appeared as the first possibility. "He wants her to pay for strippers and blow?" Wraith asked in disgust.

"They're famous for blackmail. I'd bet an hour of revenue on a Saturday night that they have something on him."

Wraith trusted Lucien's hunches. The MC president's intuition had gotten the Devil Daddies out of a lot of sticky situations before anything could happen.

"I need to pay Adam a visit. Could you send me some screenshots? I'd like to clue in Caroline's lawyer."

"On their way to your phone," Lucien assured him as he turned to focus on the computer screen.

Wraith had reached the door when Lucien spoke. "We need to ride to avenge Hellcat. Put it together for tomorrow night. Rally everyone. Skeleton crew here."

"That's going to make it tough for the staff at Inferno on a Saturday night."

"Choose carefully who stays," Lucien suggested.

"Got it."

Wraith grabbed a table in a closed section of Inferno with a view of the entrance. He wasn't sure when Caroline would arrive, but he'd keep an eye out for her. Pulling up the duty roster, he adjusted Inferno's staffing for Saturday night.

"I'm not working the front door," Razor announced, drawing his attention.

"Revenge run or checking IDs?" Wraith summed up his choices in a few words.

"Tomorrow? Lucien will insist I stay here to deal with any emergencies when the MC gets back," Razor said, running a hand through his hair.

"Exactly. You're good at the front door. I can read intentions, but you've got that fancy diploma to prove you have people radar," Wraith pointed out before adding, "Tomorrow, Inferno will be short-staffed while we're gone. Having you at the entrance will eliminate fifty percent of possible problems."

"Eighty," Razor corrected him.

"Sounds like we both think that's where you should be."

"Fuck you, Wraith."

Amused, Wraith asked, "Does that prove you have a daddy complex or a mommy one?"

"Save me from amateur psychologists," Razor grumbled and stalked away.

He wouldn't be the only one to complain to Wraith. Street appeared next. Holding up a hand to ward off the younger man's demand, Wraith said, "You want to go. I understand. I would too. Lucien's rules. No revenge rides until you've been a Devil for twelve months."

"I'm at eleven months, Wraith. That's close. I'm all in," Street said.

"You're welcome to talk to Lucien. Have him message me with his approval."

"There's no way in hell he'll do that."

"Not a chance. That's why you're not joining us. Besides, I need you at the back bar. All the hotheads gather there. We need to protect the bartenders. Can you do that?" Wraith asked, aware that Amber worked on Saturdays and Street watched her like a hawk.

"I'll do it. But I'm in the next time," the young biker said, making a last demand.

"If I decide you go," Wraith told him, meeting Street's glare with a powerful one of his own.

The standoff lasted for a few seconds before Street nodded and retreated. Wraith made a small tally mark on his scratch sheet next to Razor's. How many would he end up with by the time he finished?

"I hope you're not keeping track of the number of minutes I'm late," Caroline said, glancing at the paper in front of Wraith.

"No, Precious. I'm messing with the schedule for tomorrow night," he assured her as he stood up to hug and kiss her. "I'm glad to see you, Little girl."

"Hi, Daddy," she whispered to him before asking, "Do we have door duty on Saturday?"

"Not on Saturday. You'll be at home, snuggling with Jam. You might enjoy watching a movie on my laptop."

"I meant to ask. I've got a big TV at my place. We could bring it to your house."

"That is very sweet of you to offer it," Wraith told her.

"You don't want a TV."

"Not really. I like having all your attention when we're not working. Between playing in your room, reading, and talking, are you getting bored?"

"No. It's what everyone else does." Caroline shrugged.

"Sometimes going along with the rest of humanity isn't the best thing to do." Wraith hated the idea of zoning out in front of the TV. But perhaps she needed that escape. He'd keep an eye on her.

"Is anything wrong with the schedule?" she asked.

"No. It's all fixed now. A group is heading out for a ride tomorrow night. I needed to keep enough Devils here to manage the crowd."

"Oh, an excursion. I'll love that."

"You, Little girl, will be at the cabin safe and secure. This isn't a joyride."

"Oh."

He could tell from her expression that he'd handled that poorly. He didn't want to spook her further, but he wouldn't lie to her. "I promise to take you along with the group some other time."

"Really?"

"Yes, Precious. Another day."

"Okay. Can we grab some food before we go to the door? Maybe a hot dog and French fries?"

"You are a woman after my own heart. Want chili or boring mustard on yours?" he asked.

"Mustard is less calories," she said and wrinkled her nose.

"Two hot dogs with chili, it is. Want to come with me or wait at the table and people watch?"

"I'll stay here."

"I'll be fast," Wraith promised. Leaving the closed area, he weaved through the traffic to the bar to put their orders in and grab a couple of bottles of water. If he was right, his Little girl had forgotten to refill her tumbler while she wrote today.

He turned to meet Hellcat's furious glare. "Hey, I'm glad to see you moving around. You got out of the hospital today, right?"

"You don't have me on the list. If anyone deserves to go, it's me," Hellcat said and winced as someone ran into him accidentally.

"Tell me you didn't ride your bike to Inferno," Wraith demanded.

"Fury brought me from the hospital in a car."

"Fury did?" Wraith doubted that. The doctors would have instructed him to go home and rest.

"He threatened to walk from his cabin if I didn't drive him," Fury said from behind the angry biker.

"Hellcat, go home. If you don't, I'll bench you on the next three rides," Wraith told him. He was absolutely fed up with the amount of crap he'd gotten all day.

"You can't keep me from trailing you," Hellcat threatened.

"I can and will. Lucien will pull your membership if you don't follow protocol."

"You'd rat me out to Daddy?" Hellcat asked with sarcasm dripping from his words.

"Okay, Hellcat. So that's why the nurse forced you to sign that paper stating not to make any financial decisions for twenty-hour hours. You've lost your hold on reality. I'll drive him home, Wraith. Sorry." Fury shook his head as he grabbed Hellcat's arm.

"I don't need any help," Hellcat snapped.

"Hellcat? You're scaring me. Your face is contorted with pain. Would you go rest so you can heal?" Caroline's quiet, worried voice caused all the men to turn.

Hellcat studied her for a long minute before nodding. "I'll go home."

"Thank you. I'll cook you some chicken soup tomorrow," she promised.

"She's not making you chicken soup," Wraith bluntly told Hellcat. "I'll bring you a can, and you can suck it up. I need someone to man the gate at the complex. My thought was to see if you were up to it." He glanced deliberately toward Caroline to clue Hellcat in. Wraith wanted to ensure his Little girl was safe.

Hellcat looked up at the ceiling before nodding. "I'll man the complex."

"Thanks, Hellcat," Wraith told him. "We'll do a thorough job."

"Come on, Hellcat. Time to go home." Fury tried to take his arm, but Hellcat shook him off.

"Feel better, Hellcat," Caroline called after him.

Wraith wrapped his arm around his Little girl and hugged her close. Hellcat would never have stood down if Caroline hadn't needed his protection. It was a win-win situation.

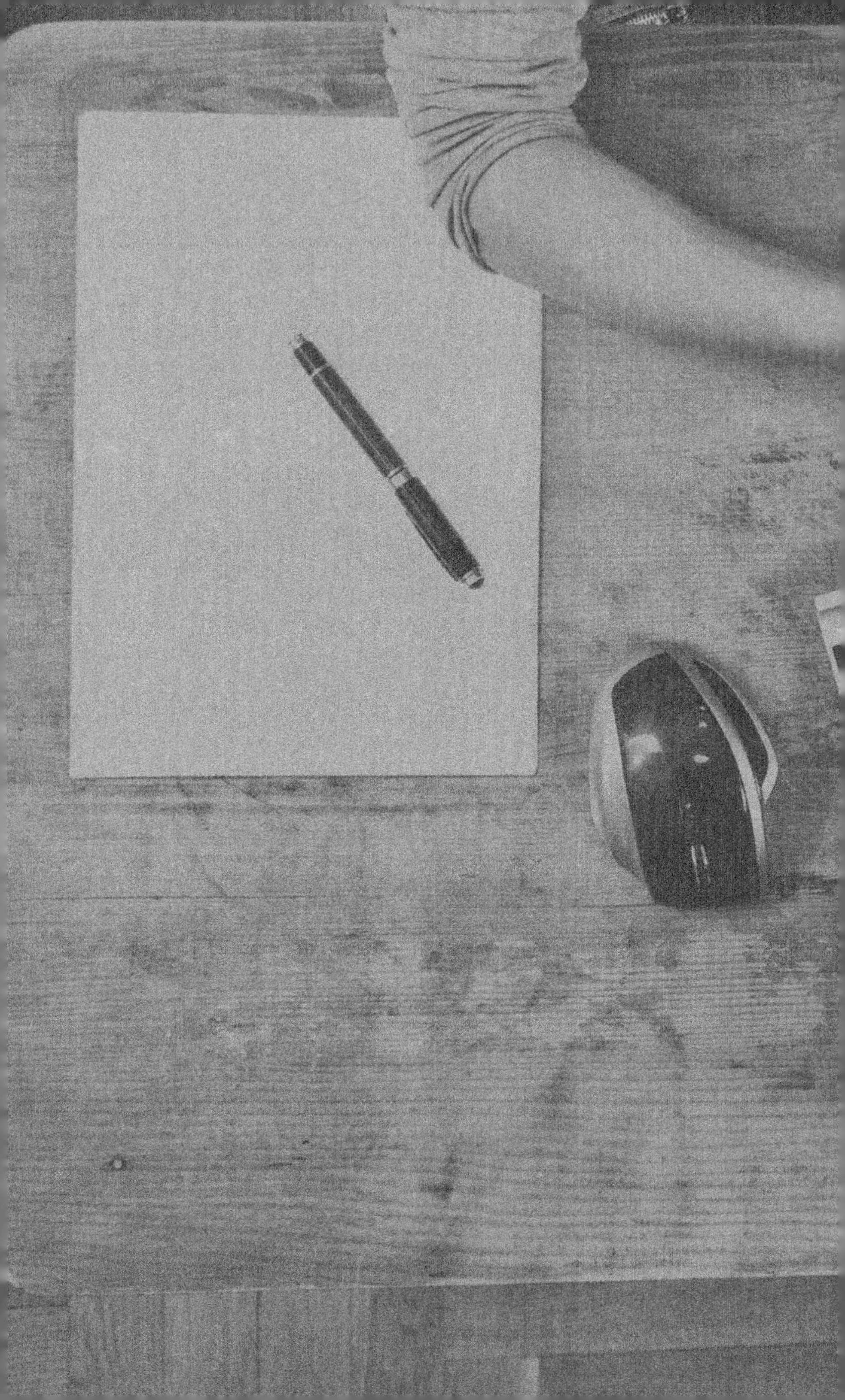

CHAPTER 14

"Hi! I'm watching a movie with Jam. I thought you might be lonely," Caroline practiced over and over as she walked up to the front of the complex with her computer and stuffie. She'd stayed at home for a half hour after Wraith left before her worries overwhelmed her.

As she got closer to the back door of the guard shack, Caroline worried she might have not thought this through well. Before she could chicken out, she made herself knock.

"What the fuck?" echoed from inside.

Caroline waved, figuring Hellcat could see her on the camera. He was at the door in thirty seconds.

"You are supposed to be tucked in safely in Wraith's cabin," Hellcat told her.

"Hi! I'm watching a movie with Jam and figured you'd be lonely," she recited almost perfectly.

When he stared at her, Caroline's brave face crumbled. "The cabins are abandoned, and the wind is whipping around, making all sorts of noises. I'm scared. Besides, I thought you'd get the word that everyone was okay first. Can I wait with you?"

Hellcat stared at her for what seemed like an eternity before stepping back and waving her inside. "Come in. It's better that you stay with me than wander in the dark. What movie are we watching?"

"You like cats, right?"

"I do," he answered.

"You get to choose—old or new?" Caroline set her computer on the table under the windows, flipped open the screen, and showed him the two choices. "Old or new?" she repeated, pointing from one to the other.

"New. I haven't seen that."

"You'll love it. It's awesome!" She busied herself pulling the film up and starting it while he grabbed another chair up to join him. Caroline settled in that one comfortably and glanced over at him. "Thanks for letting me in."

"You're welcome. I needed to meet Jelly, anyway."

"His name is Jam." Caroline rushed to correct him.

"Of course. My apologies, Jam."

Coming up here was a good idea. So much better than listening to every sound inside and outside the cabin with Jam. The purple monkey didn't want to admit he was scared too, but Caroline had felt him shaking.

As the first notes of the music sounded, she focused back on the screen. About an hour into the movie, Hellcat tensed beside her.

"Caroline, slide out of your chair to sit on the floor. I want you out of sight," Hellcat snapped as he closed the top of her laptop, silencing the show.

Without asking any questions, Caroline followed his directions. The urgency in his voice alone scared her. She squeezed into the smallest space possible under the desk, hugging Jam close to reassure him. Headlights flashed over the ceiling of the shack. Hellcat pulled a gun out of his leather cut, and she swallowed hard.

"Damn. I hoped he was making a U-turn. Stay quiet," Hellcat told her under his breath.

Caroline could hear the powerful engine as it pulled up to

the window. Hellcat hit an intercom button and snarled, "You're on private property. Turn around and head back to the main road."

"Hey, sorry to bother you. My wife must have broken down around here. I haven't heard from her for a couple of hours, so I tracked her car to this location. She's about five hundred feet past the entrance."

Caroline recognized that voice. Adam. What was he doing? And the asshole had a tracker in her car?

"No wives here. Turn around." Hellcat's tone didn't invite a conversation.

"Now, that's not very helpful. I'd hate to get the police involved," Adam threatened in a polite tone.

"You are welcome to call them from the public road. I've told you twice already to turn around. Do that now." Hellcat stood from his seat. He lifted his right hand and set it on the table in Adam's view. The barrel of his gun shone under the fluorescent lights.

Caroline could tell the previously injured biker was still moving with pain, but Adam wouldn't pick up on that. Hellcat outmuscled her ex by a huge percentage. And he was armed. She held her breath. How far was Adam going to push this?

"Gotcha. One more thing before I leave. My wife lives in a land of make-believe filled with knights in shining armor and damsels in distress. She suffers from delusions and is easily confused. Some might consider allowing her to stay the same as kidnapping."

Uh-oh. He's becoming angry. Caroline could hear the frustration in Adam's tone. He didn't make good choices when he didn't get his way.

A rumble from the road caught Caroline's attention. Were the Devils on their way back? She smirked. It really sucked to be Adam.

"I'll head out. Keep my warning in mind," her ex stated with bravado.

Caroline peeked out of her safe spot and caught Hellcat's slow, lethal smile.

The roaring engine sounds now came from outside the guard shack. Caroline peeked out the side window to see motorcycles surrounding Adam's beloved sports car. She recognized the man who swung his leg over his bike by his sheer mass alone. Two more bikers dismounted to flank him.

Wraith strolled up to Adam's window. He didn't address him but stared at him as he asked Hellcat. "Who's this piece of shit who can't read 'no trespassing' signs?"

"Says he's tracked his wife here. She's delusional and mentally ill," Hellcat shared. Caroline noticed he didn't exit the guard shack. She guessed he was concerned Adam would spot her.

"What's her name?" Wraith asked.

"Caroline McConnell. She's got brown hair and eyes. Could lose thirty pounds or so. You know how women are when they get married—always eating," Adam joked, obviously trying to bond with Wraith.

She rolled those brown eyes and shook her head. A loud metallic snap made her freeze.

"What the hell?" Adam didn't sound happy.

"Whoops! That was clumsy of me," Wraith acknowledged. "They don't attach side mirrors like they used to."

"Hellcat? How many times did you tell this guy to leave?" Wraith asked, never taking his eyes off Adam.

"Three, Wraith."

"Oh, in that case." A second crunch followed.

"Fuck!" Adam yelled.

Caroline put Jam over her mouth. That must be the other mirror.

"That's two. Windshield or rear window?" Wraith asked.

"Hey. I get the message. I'll leave if you'll move the bikes around me," Adam told him.

Glass shattering told her the bikers had administered the third consequence.

"Devils, better shift your bikes. I doubt if this guy drives well on a good day. He's never coming back here. Whoever his wife is, he's going to speak much nicer about her in the future. Because if he harasses her in any way, this conversation will move from pleasant to angry. I don't think he's going to enjoy that."

Caroline gritted her teeth together to keep from giggling. Adam's skills in manipulating people didn't work on Wraith and the Devil Daddies. She hadn't thought she'd see Adam slammed with consequences for being a total jerk to her. It felt incredibly good to have others see through his crap.

Adam sat quietly in his car as the Devils shifted their bikes into the complex. Wraith didn't budge from his spot next to her ex's window. Caroline saw the imposing man lean forward to speak to Adam privately. She couldn't hear what he said and decided maybe she didn't want to.

"Looks like you lost a fight. Maybe I don't need to worry about you if I'm not outnumbered ten to one," Adam answered.

Instantly concerned that Wraith was injured, Caroline shifted, rising from her sheltered spot on the floor. Hellcat moved his hand with lightning speed to stop her, pinning her out of sight. He squeezed slightly to warn her. Caroline knew a few minutes delay wouldn't hurt Wraith any more, but she wasn't happy waiting.

"You have no idea how battered the other side is," Wraith pointed out. "They won't mess with one of ours. And you won't return. Back up. The road is clear behind you."

A squeal of tires on the road told her how quickly Adam followed her Daddy's instructions. Caroline tried to stand, but Hellcat held her in place. "Not yet," he hissed.

When his grip relaxed, she rose to her feet and bolted out the door. She skidded to a halt in front of Wraith and stared at his bruised face. "What happened? Are you okay?"

"Come give me a hug, Precious. I'm fine. Much better than when I figured out you were in the guard shack with Hellcat instead of safe in my cabin," Wraith said, leveling a stern glance at her.

"Ummm. Could we talk about it at the cabin?"

"You bet," Wraith assured her.

Caroline dashed into the guard shack to grab her laptop and Jam. She whispered to Hellcat, "Thanks for keeping me company. We'll finish the movie next time. You won't believe how it ends."

"I'll look forward to it," Hellcat assured her before turning to Wraith. "She was scared, Wraith. The wind has been wicked loud."

"I'll consider that. Thanks for keeping her safe. Sullivan's crew won't bother shipments anymore. We came to an agreement. The guys can explain more."

Wraith opened his saddlebag for Caroline to stash her laptop and Jam inside. After unfastening his helmet, he strapped it on Caroline. "Let's go home, Precious."

"What about you?" she whispered, touching his helmet.

"I'll make it safely to the cabin," he promised as he started the bike.

Caroline slid awkwardly into place, wondering if she'd ever get better at hopping on and off the massive bike. Wrapping her arms around Wraith, she rested her head on his back and relaxed. He was safe.

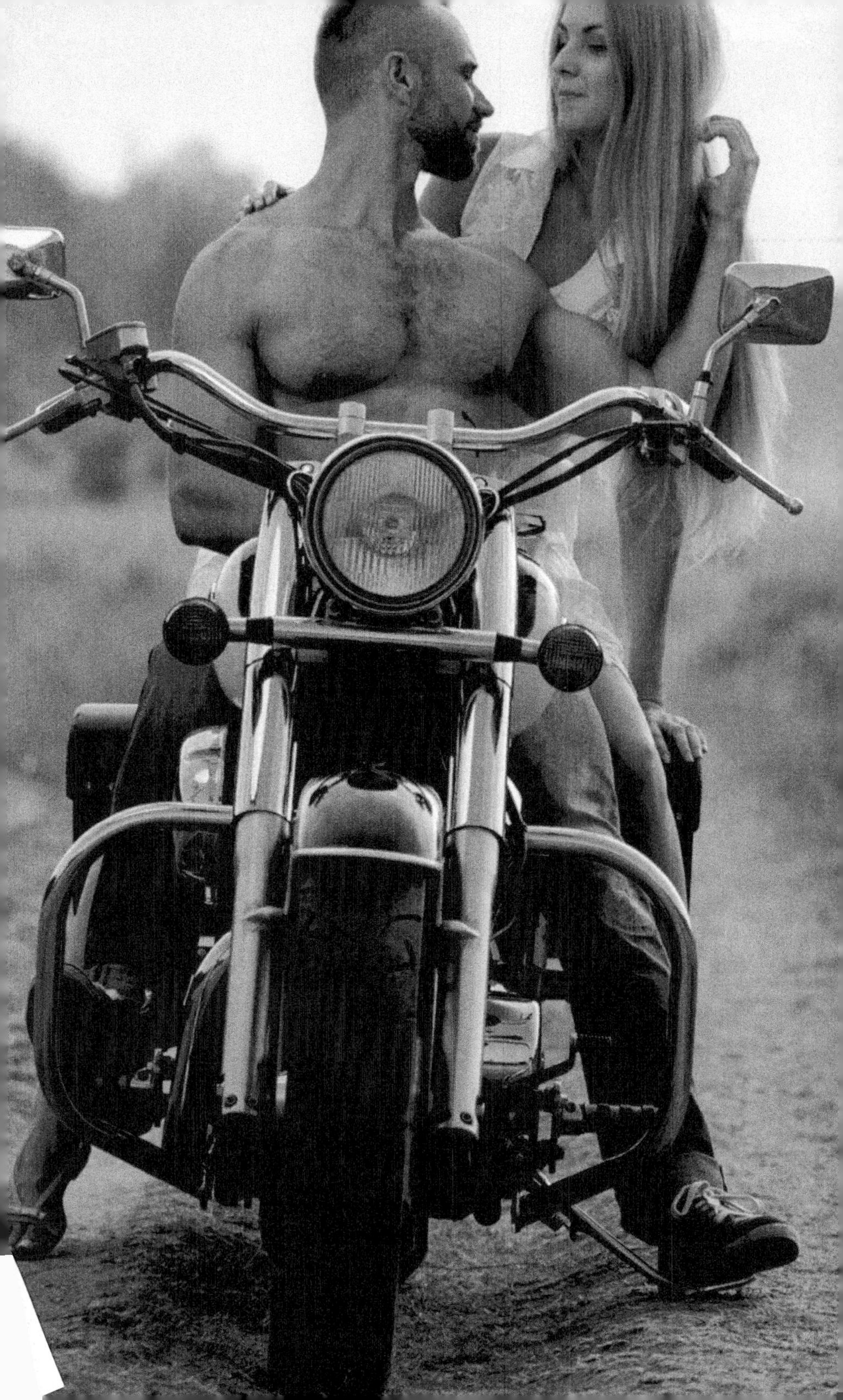

CHAPTER 15

"Sorry!" Wraith wrapped his arm around Caroline and escorted her inside. "I'm sorry you were scared. Going up to stay with Hellcat wasn't the best idea. That could have been dangerous."

"I realized that when Adam showed up." She rushed forward to touch her fingertips to a bruise on his cheek. "You're hurt. We need to get something cold on this before it swells."

He allowed her to tow him into the kitchen and sat on the stool Caroline pointed to. Wraith enjoyed watching her flit around his kitchen to clean up his cuts and fuss over him. When she opened a drawer, he suspected she intended to make him an ice bag. "Put those cubes in a glass for me instead," he suggested.

"Like for whisky?" she suggested. "If you have a blender, I can concoct a piña colada. It would be frosty and cool on your mouth."

"I'm not drinking a froufrou drink, Little girl. You can make yourself *one* if you'd like to join me." He stressed that he'd only allow her a drink as he rose to grab a bottle of bourbon from the top cabinet and a rocks glass.

"I could have some of that," she suggested, pointing at the bottle in his hand.

Setting the bottle down, Wraith reached for another glass and held both out to Caroline. "Two ice cubes in mine, please."

She leaned over to get ice from the dispenser in the bottom freezer drawer. Wraith enjoyed the view of her plump bottom and created a plan for later. A vision of Caroline on her knees in front of him popped into his mind. *Yeah, that will happen.* He imagined that as he splashed bourbon into each glass.

He handed her the drink and waited as she lifted it to her lush mouth. She swallowed, and he watched her throat move as the fiery liquid descended.

"Mmm." She hummed with enjoyment.

She was full of surprises, and he loved them all. *Love?* That rocked him back to the cabinet. Could he love her already? *Yeah.*

He'd known she was in the guard shack after catching a glimpse of her computer on the desk. Caroline wouldn't let it get out of her sight. Very little scared Wraith. He could stare down a giant man towering over him. The thought that she could be in danger had ignited anxiety inside him. She was incredibly special.

"What's wrong? You look like you've been hit by a sack of potatoes."

"No potatoes."

"Did everything go okay? Are they going to leave Hellcat alone? What do they have against him anyway?"

Wraith smiled and winced when it pulled his cut lip. He rolled the side of his glass over it, enjoying the cold sensation on his swollen mouth. "There's an ancient sack of frozen peas in the freezer. Would you grab that for me?"

"Of course!"

Another great view. Wraith adjusted himself slightly as his jeans got tighter. When she whirled back around to hand him the battered plastic bag, he said, "Thanks, Precious. Let's go sit down, and I can answer your questions."

"Thank you."

Settling onto the couch with a sigh of delight, Wraith guided her onto his lap. This was the life. Good bourbon, an adorable Little, and the opportunity to enjoy both.

"So?" she asked.

"Hellcat was in the wrong place at the wrong time. He didn't do anything wrong. That group was out to disrupt the transport, and Hellcat just happened to get that load."

"What was in it? Were they trying to steal it?"

"There are some things I can't tell you, Little girl. And yes, I'm sure they would have taken the truck if Hellcat wasn't such a tough guy."

"Did they have guns tonight?"

"It's probably better if you don't worry about that," he told her.

"Do you ever drive a truck out?"

"I've been on runs before—trucks, cars, vans—pretty much everything. Now, I'm more useful to Lucien around the warehouse so I don't haul loads anymore."

Caroline took a sip of her bourbon, eying him over the rim. "Is what you're doing illegal?"

"It would depend who you ask, Little girl."

"That's very cryptic. You can't give me a straight answer?" she probed.

"The world isn't always black and white, Caroline. I wouldn't work for Lucien if I didn't believe what he's doing is right."

"Do all the Devil Daddies work there?"

"No, Precious. There are men from many different walks of life who belong to the MC. The guys you'll see the most are those who hold positions in the warehouse or help at Inferno."

"That makes sense." Caroline finished her bourbon and handed the glass to Wraith. She curled up on his chest and closed her eyes.

Wraith grabbed her blanket from the back of the couch where

she must have abandoned it when she took off for the guard shack. He draped it over her lap. While she was at the cabin, Caroline didn't stray too far from the soft fabric. It often flopped on him at night when she turned over with it held in her hand.

"Thanks, Daddy. I'm glad you're home," she told him before yawning.

"Me too."

As she relaxed, he replayed the fight that night. Hellcat's attackers were part of a crime ring that operated out of the bad side of town. Wraith would start altering routes, especially for the most important loads, to avoid their territory. Not abandoning it completely, of course. Wraith didn't want them to get the idea that the Devils were scared of them. They'd maintain their presence but not offer anything too tempting.

When he heard a small snore coming from Caroline, Wraith knew he should get her in the shower and then under the covers. He didn't have any energy to mess with that. Not yet. He'd savor holding her as she slept.

An hour later, he rallied his energy to put her to bed. Lifting her in his arms, Wraith carried Caroline to their bedroom and into the large bathroom. Setting her feet on the floor, he steadied her.

"Let Daddy get you undressed, Precious."

"No, Daddy. I'm sleeping," she protested, rubbing her eyes.

"I know." Wraith reassured her with a kiss on her forehead. She cooperated as he stripped off her clothing. Cooperating might be the exact description for her actions. Half-asleep, Caroline bonked her nose twice and almost fell over a few times. Finally, he had her naked and adorably drowsy.

"Baby, I need you to stand next to the vanity for a minute while I get rid of my clothes too." He leaned her against the marble top and stepped away to pull his T-shirt over his head.

As he tossed it into the hamper, she muttered, "It's cold, Daddy. My butt's freezing."

Wraith smiled at her delayed reaction before consoling her,

"I'm sorry, Precious. We'll take a hot shower and warm up." He moved to the large enclosure and turned on the water to heat.

"Good idea," she said, wrapping her arms around herself.

As he stepped out of his shoes, she watched him undressing with an unfocused gaze. "You're warm."

"Thank you, Little girl. Did you by chance have anything to drink in the guard shack tonight?" She hadn't seemed intoxicated earlier.

"No, Daddy. I only had one bourbon with you. I'm wiped out. Maybe I could get some energy back," she suggested, staring as he pushed his jeans over his hips.

"Going nite-nite sounds like a very good thing for you."

"Will you wrap yourself around me and keep me and Jam toasty?"

"Of course. Come on, Precious. In the shower. Let's get wet."

"Can I let you in on a secret, Daddy?"

Before he could tell her yes, Caroline continued in a loud whisper. "I'm already wet."

Wraith urged his junk not to listen as he guided Caroline into the shower stall. The annoying aches from the fight faded quickly from his mind. Especially with the heated water flooding over him. *Get in, get cleaned, get in bed.*

"I'll do your back, Daddy," she volunteered, scooting around him.

Her full breasts dragged across his arm and back, wiping a portion of his resolve away. He dropped his face into the spray to distract himself as her hands rubbed silky liquid soap over his skin. Damn, that felt good. He kept the words inside, trying not to encourage her, but the Little minx expanded her cleaning efforts to his butt.

"You're playing with fire, Precious."

"I'm okay with that," she answered, but returned to cleaning his back.

He noticed the sleepiness had faded from her voice. Lifting his arms over his head, Wraith rotated, allowing her hands to slide over his torso. He trapped her in his embrace and pulled her close, lowering his head to capture her mouth. Her response was energetic, fueling his desire.

"Mmm," he hummed against her lips. She tasted like bourbon and her own sweet flavor. It was addictive. No, she was addictive.

Wraith stepped closer, crowding her to the tiled wall. Her fingers tightened on his shoulders. The prick of her fingernails into his skin pushed his arousal higher. He loved it when she lost control.

In an attempt to focus, he dispensed bodywash into his hand and smoothed it over her. The silkiness of her wet skin and the thick lather fueled his desire. Cupping her breasts, he spread the soap over her sensitive peaks and inhaled her small gasps of delight with his kisses. Abandoning those prizes, he glided his hands down her torso to her pussy.

She'd told him the truth. Her pussy was slick with arousal. That deserved a reward, right? Wraith caressed her, exploring her pink folds before spreading the lather back between her cheeks. Caroline bucked away from his fingers and directly toward his burgeoning erection, drawing a gasp from her and an aroused moan from him.

"Daddy, not there," she whispered against his lips.

"Nothing is off-limits to me, Little girl. I will enjoy making love to you here soon."

"No, Daddy. I've never…."

"Don't tell Daddy no. I'll help you get ready, so you'll love having me fill your bottom," he promised, poking his fingertip into her small entrance. Her shimmy against him completely invalidated her frantic headshaking. Wraith could feel her slick juices gushing over his cock as her imagination went into overdrive.

He needed to be buried inside her now. "Come on, Precious. Let's get rinsed. I have plans for you."

In a flurry of caresses and trips under the spray, Wraith got all the suds removed from their bodies. He flipped off the water and towel-dried them off. Wraith wasn't going to make it to bed. Guiding her over to the sink, he crowded behind her, pressing her torso to the marble top. Caroline gasped as her nipples grazed the cold surface and scooted backward, lifting her full bottom toward him.

He ground his erection against her, drawing a gasp from her lips. Her head lifted to meet his gaze in the mirror. Wraith loved the way her expression changed from surprised to aroused as she took in how he'd positioned her. Pressing her firmly to the vanity, Wraith then stroked her from neck to spine. He settled his cock at the entrance of her drenched opening.

"Watch me fuck you, Little girl."

Immediately, he thrust inside, filling her completely. Her head reared back as her mouth rounded in an O as he held himself deep inside her. She pulsed around him, testing his control. The warm, velvety grasp of her tight channel was sinfully delicious.

"Please move," she begged, rocking backward.

His mouth curved in a wolfish grin that looked dangerous even to him in the mirror. He gripped her full hips and moved. Withdrawing from her, Wraith slammed back into her heat. This time, he didn't pause. He couldn't go slow.

Their bodies crashed together. Each sensation tested his control. He wouldn't last long. Wrapping his arm around her, Wraith explored her wetness to find her clit. He brushed his fingertip across it as he moved inside her.

Caroline's body clamped around him as she moaned, "Daddy."

"Good girl," he praised, continuing his caresses as he quickened his strokes. Her climax intensified, spasming around him. Wraith relaxed his control and flooded her. Caroline cried out, joining his orgasm with a second burst of pleasure.

Dropping to his forearms, Wraith draped himself over her. He allowed her to feel a small portion of his weight pinning her to the vanity top as he pressed soft kisses to her neck and shoulders. "You are such a treasure, Caroline."

"Mmm," she hummed in contentment as she recovered.

When he could move, Wraith cleaned them both up before carrying her into the bedroom to tuck her into the covers. He rounded the bed to climb in and saw her hand searching between their pillows. "I'll go get Jam, Precious."

"And blankie?" she asked drowsily.

"And blankie."

When he returned, she'd snuggled into his pillow. Enchanted, Wraith set her stuffie and blanket next to her chest before wrapping himself around her. They could both sleep on his side tonight.

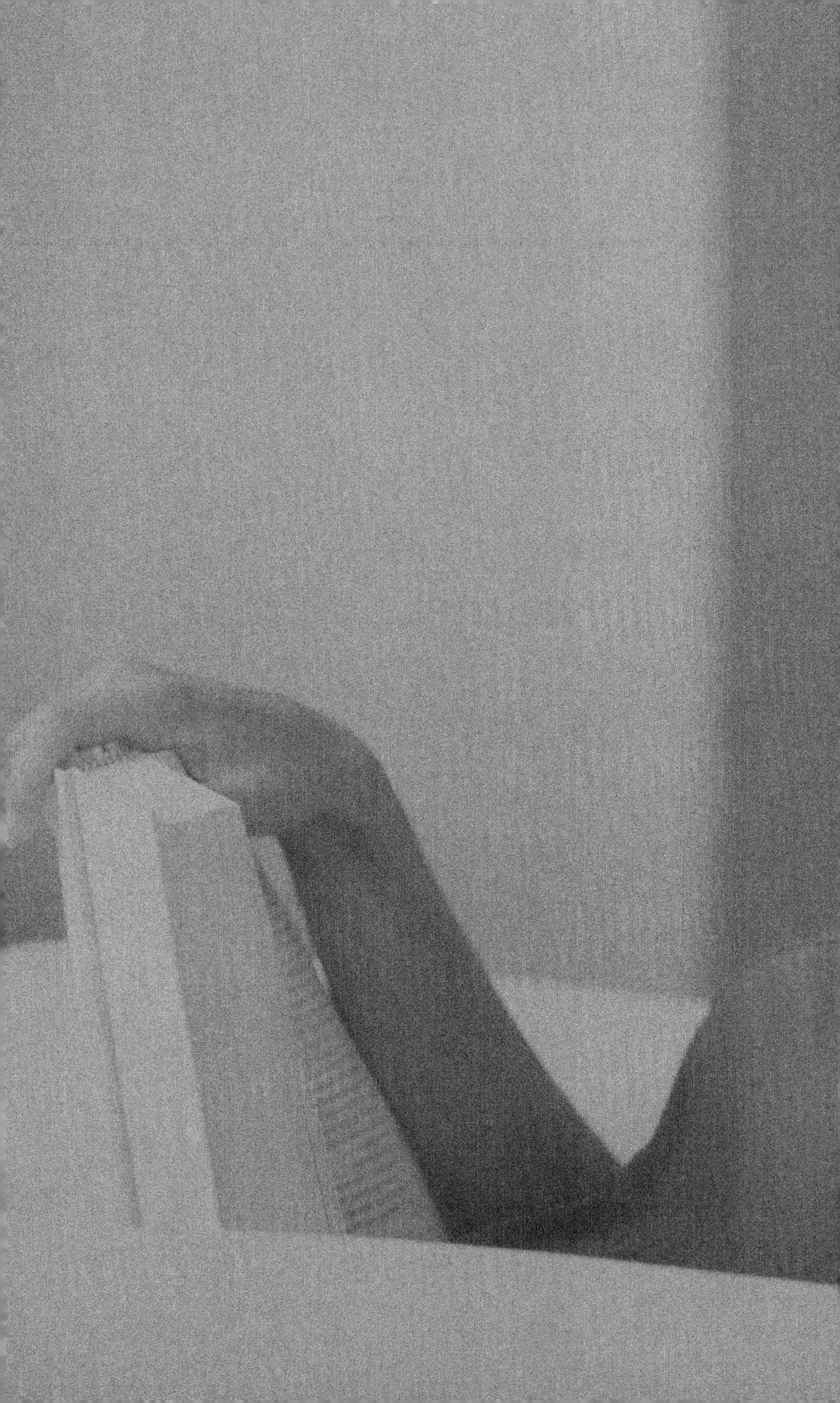

CHAPTER 16

Life had been quiet since the Devils had turned away her ex at the gate. Wraith had found a tracker in her trunk. He'd allowed her to choose how to dispose of it. Caroline hoped Adam was still chasing Inferno's produce delivery van around town.

Caroline loved typing in Wraith's remote cabin. She'd gotten a lot of writing done there. And a lot of inspiration for certain scenes in those books—like the morning after their sex on the vanity when he'd placed an anal dilator in her bottom before leaving for work.

That happened now on a regular basis. If she cooperated, he'd kiss her goodbye after plugging her and drawing a quick orgasm from her. Wraith could play her like a concert pianist. He got her.

Caroline loved falling back to sleep, all flushed with excitement. Wraith had established the rule that she had to call him before removing it. He sometimes said no. She loved his control. Just thinking about it made her shiver.

When her phone buzzed and Daddy appeared on her screen, Caroline smiled. Wraith had removed his name and replaced it with that title. She answered and clicked on the speaker.

"Hi, Daddy. I've got my word count done. Can I come to Inferno this evening?"

"Not tonight, Caroline. I think you need some Little time with Daddy alone in the cabin." His gravelly voice alone would have sent a thrill through her, but his message made her heart beat faster.

"Little time?" she repeated.

"Yes. I think we need to enjoy your nursery. I left a special outfit laid out on your changing table. Have you noticed it?"

She jumped to her feet and headed that way. "No. I've been focused on work. I haven't played today."

Caroline stopped in the doorway at the sight of the clothes displayed for her. Slowly, she advanced into the room. Touching the soft fabric, she admired the beautiful, soft rose shade. "The dress is beautiful," she told her Daddy.

"I think you will look lovely in that color," he told her softly. "Don't put it on. Daddy will do that for you. Are you ready to close down your computer for the day?"

"Yes, Daddy."

"Go do that and then if you'd like, you hang out in your nursery until I get home."

"Are you on your way?" she asked, hearing the background noise change from the warehouse echoing with voices and big machinery to the wind blowing into the speaker.

"I'm getting ready to put on my helmet. I'll be home soon, Little girl."

"Okay, Daddy. I'm excited for you to get here. Um…."

"You can tell me, Precious. Is something bothering you?"

"I'm nervous."

"Of course you are, and that's okay. Trying something new can be exciting and scary, but I'll be with you."

"Okay, Daddy," she whispered. "See you soon."

After disconnecting the call, she rubbed the soft fabric between her fingers. Caroline would love the dress even if it was short. It was the other things that made her worry. Her Daddy had set a pull-up from the shelf underneath next to the dress with a matching ruffled diaper cover. She traced a flouncy decoration, loving how cute it was.

Pulling her bravery around her like a cloak, she poked the pull-up. It crinkled slightly, and she suspected it would make noise when she moved. Darling ducklings danced along the front. Would he want her to use it?

Her gaze slid over the new package of wipes, a tube of diaper cream, and a container of powder that had appeared on the side organizer. She tried to ignore the large tub of lubricant and a thick thermometer, but her bottom clinched. Her Daddy consistently widened that small entrance with plugs. He'd mentioned checking her temperature before. Her gaze landed on thick bands at the sides of the changing table. She saw more at the top. The loops were designed to hold something in place. Restraints. Those were new.

Caroline shimmied back from the changing table. She clasped her hands together to keep from wringing them. Her Daddy had promised he wouldn't force her to try things more than three times. But he didn't let her lie to herself either. She'd protested the anal dilators a lot in the beginning but had to admit she found them arousing.

Her panties were already wet. He'd know she was excited when he changed her clothes. She could go put on a fresh pair of underwear, but she had her Wednesday panties on that he had laid out for her to put on that morning. That would be a dead giveaway that she was trying to fool him. He wouldn't like that.

She needed Jam. Running to the bedroom, she found her stuffie and quickly explained the situation. He treated her to the biggest hug and demanded to see her new outfit. She carried him with her to the nursery and waited impatiently as he checked out the items on the table. Jam gave her that look. He had a secret to tell her. Setting his mouth next to her ear, she listened closely.

"You're going to have fun."

Pulling him away so she could study his face, Caroline stared at him for a few seconds. What a great way to think of the activities her Daddy had planned—as play! That helped lighten her anxiety. Wraith was an amazing Daddy. He always listened to her and made sure she was happy and comfortable with their play. That wouldn't change when he helped her be super Little.

Caroline hugged the purple monkey to her chest. It was so good to have a friend. Maybe someday another one of the guys in the compound would find his Little. Or would that be frightening as well? Was there a right way to be Little?

"Did I scare you, Precious?" Wraith's deep voice drew her out of her speculation.

Racing to his side, she cuddled close to his chest as he hugged her tight. "Hi, Daddy. Jam helped me not worry. Then I thought about what would happen if another Devil moved someone special in with him."

"Oh, like a friend you could play with in your nursery? I bet you would love that. There used to be a few guys here with Littles. They had a blast together. Unfortunately, people have to relocate a lot these days for work, family, or other reasons. Let's keep our fingers crossed that someone else is as lucky as I am soon."

"They might not like me," she whispered.

"Caroline, let me tell you a secret. Littles are the best people. They are sweet to others and love being themselves. I'd bet twenty bucks you'd be buddies in five minutes."

"Twenty whole dollars? That's a steep bid," she teased.

"Are you poking fun at your Daddy?" he asked and tickled her ribcage, making her giggle.

"Daddy! Stop!" she begged and when he relented immediately, hugged him close.

"I guess we'll see when your new bestie arrives who's right," Wraith told her with a wink. "Are you ready to let Daddy see how cute you are in the new things he picked up for you?"

Caroline nodded and leaned against him, needing his

strength to make her brave. His large hand rubbed up and down her spine, reassuring her. Caroline met his gaze and whispered, "You'll help me?"

"Always, Little girl. That's what Daddies do. Come on, let's put these big girl clothes away."

He stripped off her simple T-shirt and leggings and tossed them aside before unfastening her bra. When Caroline exhaled in relief, he rubbed along the band marks and rolled her full breasts in his hands. "I'm going to make a no-bra rule. We'll get you some supportive tank tops or sports bras that don't torture you. When you're at home writing, there's no need to be uncomfortable."

"That sounds nice, Daddy. What do I wear under my dress today?"

"Little girls get to skip a lot of things when they're in their nurseries or home with their Daddies. I think that soft fabric will feel good," he suggested, brushing his fingers across her nipples.

She nodded, enjoying his attentions.

"No panties either," he announced, sliding her Wednesday cotton panties down her legs. "So wet, Caroline. Did you touch yourself while Daddy was gone?"

Shaking her head vigorously, Caroline denied the act. "I've been good."

He lifted the fabric to his nose and inhaled. "We'll get you cleaned up and fresh before you put on your outfit. I noticed when I walked in that you were flushed. Are you feeling okay?"

"Oh, yes! I'm super. Healthy, that is."

"I'll check on that. Little girls need their temperature monitored regularly," he told her as he moved the items on the changing table. "All right. Let's get you up here."

Wraith lifted her easily from the floor and helped her stretch out on the table. He wrapped a thick belt across her ribcage. "I don't want you to roll off. Let me have your hands, Caroline. I can tell you're nervous. Daddy will take care of you."

He lifted her arms over her head and attached them to the top of the table. "Now, Daddy's in charge."

Caroline sighed in relief. She didn't have to make any decisions. That eased her anxiety. Choosing to be super Little was scary. Now, it was all on Daddy's broad shoulders. She assessed his strength as he leaned over her. Wraith wouldn't have any trouble supporting her.

"Let's turn you over on your side, Caroline." He rolled her easily to face the wall. When she settled, he bent her knees up and secured her calves. "I think we need some decorations in front of you on the wall. What should we add to the room?"

Shivering as he ran his hand over her side and bottom, Caroline knew what was coming next. She forced herself to concentrate on his question. "I like snails, Daddy."

"Hmm," he mused as he opened the lid of something below her knees. She couldn't see what he was doing. Her legs blocked her view. She could only imagine.

"Like escargot to munch on?" His question drew her attention to him.

"No, Daddy. Cute snails with their houses on their backs."

"Oh, I see. This may be cold for a minute," he warned as he lifted her buttock and spread something slippery over her puckered entrance before pressing inside to apply it to her inner walls like he did when she had to wear a plug.

This time, when he removed his fingers, he inserted a long tube deep into her bottom. The thermometer. Wraith twirled it in her bottom, seating it deeper until he covered the end with his hand that rested on her skin. "Five minutes, Little girl. We'll make sure you feel well enough to continue. Tell me what you created today."

"I wrote a sex scene in the shower. It was steamy."

"I'll look forward to reading that. Do we need to recreate it?" he asked.

"We already did, Daddy. Well, with some changes. I wouldn't write what we do in my books exactly."

"I'm glad, Caroline. Some activities are special between Little girls and their Daddies. Is that what made your panties wet?"

She was quiet for a few seconds before admitting in a rush, "It was the clothes and the other things."

"Seeing the tools Daddy will use to take care of you?" he asked.

"Yes." She nodded, happy he understood.

"You'll be easier to keep dry in your pull-up. Have you worn one before or used it?"

"No, Daddy."

"It's wonderful that we get to try things out together, isn't it? Two more minutes. Let's sing a song for Jam." He started a popular song that played often on the radio. She joined him, loving how he always made everything fun. They were on the last chorus when he removed the thermometer and checked her temperature.

"All good, Little girl. Let's get you cleaned up, and we'll have some playtime."

He unfastened her legs and rotated her to settle on her back. Pressing her knees far apart, he held her legs apart with powerful hands on her thighs. "Can you keep your legs here for Daddy or do you want me to restrain you?"

"Better help me, Daddy. I'm pretty nervous still."

"I gotcha, Precious." In a few seconds, he had her calves attached to the opposite sides. He paused, admiring her naked curves now exposed completely to his view. "Damn, you're pretty. Daddy's going to snap a picture of you. He promises never to show it to anyone. Do you trust me?"

"Yes, Daddy." Her juices welled from her body as he captured several pictures of her. She noticed when he slid the camera back in his back pocket, Wraith adjusted himself in his jeans.

"How wet you are. Let's get you all tidied up." She tried not to react as he stroked the wipes over her skin. It was so hard because he was very thorough around her clit and between her buttocks.

On edge, she asked, "Can I come, please?"

"If you're good, Daddy will make love to you after playtime." He unfastened the bonds around her legs and hands before lifting her down from the table.

"I'll be very good," she promised.

"You always are, Precious."

Wraith lowered himself to one knee in front of her and instructed, "Put your hand on my shoulder for balance, Little girl. Step into your pull-up. Now the other foot." He raised them up her legs to settle into place around her waist before running his hand along the crotch to make sure it was snug to her pussy.

"Those fit perfectly. Now, the cute ruffles. I can't wait to see those."

Caroline felt so cute in the ruffled panties. Wraith obviously adored them. He kept running his hand over the wavy decorations.

"We're getting these in every color," he declared. "Dress, next."

The fabric caressed her nipples. She loved it. "Can I go see what I look like?" she asked, pointing to the closet door that hid a full-length mirror inside.

"Let me do your hair first," Wraith requested.

When he opened the door a few minutes later, Caroline gasped. She loved her outfit. Twirling, she checked herself out from all angles. The dress was short, revealing most of her thighs and barely covering her panties. The final embellishment was a wide satin ribbon that ran under her breast and tied in the back. A princess stared back at her. And her hair? He'd braided it on each side and tied matching bows.

"You're as cute as a snail, Little girl."

"I'm as cute as a snail," she echoed in amazement.

"Let's play, sweetheart. You pick out something for us to do. I'm going to grab a couple of drinks for us."

Caroline twirled in front of the mirror a few more times before running over to open the toy box. She grabbed her favorite board game and sat down to set it up. With a twinkle in her eye, Caroline decided to bolster her odds of gaining victory. She moved quickly and smoothed her dress back into place as her Daddy returned. He handed her a sippy cup and set a bottle next to the rocking chair before joining her at the small table with a can of soda.

He'll never figure it out....

CHAPTER 17

Wraith sat back in his chair to stare at his Little girl in delight. She'd beaten him soundly. Who could have guessed that inside that cute enchantress lurked a board game shark? She celebrated by draining the last of her juice and slamming the sippy cup on the table before rising to her feet to twirl. He would definitely be buying more play clothes for her.

Wait! What was that? Wraith controlled his expression.

"Beat you, Daddy!" she crowed.

"I see that, Caroline. Did you cheat?" he asked casually.

She donned a comically shocked expression. "Cheat? Not me!"

"I didn't see a few extra wild cards tucked under your dress?" he asked with a raised eyebrow.

Caroline's hand went automatically to tug on the hem. "No. I wouldn't do that!"

"Come here, Precious. Daddy wants to check for himself."

She stared at him for exactly three seconds before darting toward the door. Wraith was on her trail before she'd taken three steps. He caught her in the hall and wrapped an arm around her waist to lift her off her feet. Carrying her back into the nursery, he grabbed Jam from the table where she'd abandoned him along with her blankie. She'd need them. With both tucked under his arm, Wraith walked over to the rocking chair and sat down, standing her between his legs. He held her securely in place.

"Stop trying to run, Little girl. The jig is up. Take Jam. He wants you to hold him."

Draping the blanket over the arm of the rocker, he waited for her to claim her stuffie and hug the purple monkey. "How many of those wild cards did you tuck away before I returned?"

"What are you talking about? I need to go to the bathroom, Daddy. I'll be right back."

"Not happening. It's time for this dress to come off."

"No, Daddy. I love it. I'd like to wear it for a while more."

Wraith gave her a stern glance and stripped it over her head, easily overpowering her attempts to foil his efforts while juggling the stuffie. He tossed it away and scanned her delicious form. "And what would these be?" he asked, plucking two cards from the top of her ruffled diaper cover.

"How did those get in there? Do you do magic tricks, Daddy? That's the only way they could have gotten there." Her expression was guarded, as if she were waiting to see if he'd fall for that.

"I may know some methods to coax an orgasm from you, Little girl, but I haven't mastered any card tricks," he answered.

"Maybe you have talents you haven't figured out?"

"Caroline. You realize every lie that comes out of your mouth will result in punishment, right?"

"I don't want a spanking, Daddy!" Tears gathered in her eyes, and he knew Caroline had realized she'd pushed her luck.

"Perhaps there's a better punishment for a Little girl who hoodwinked her Daddy." Wraith released her with one hand, and instantly, she attempted to twist away. He easily contained that effort. "Each time you try to run makes this worse for you, Caroline."

"Sorry," she said and pushed a trembling bottom lip out.

Steeling himself from responding to the precious sight, Wraith reached for the drawer in the table next to the rocker. He extracted a wand vibrator and set it down next to her bottle.

"What are you going to do with that?" she asked.

"You'll see. First, these cute panties need to come off. Only well-behaved Little girls get to wear these." He stripped them down her legs and helped Caroline step out of them. Leaving her pull-up on, he turned her around and lifted her onto his lap, sitting sideways on his thighs.

"Am I going to get a spanking?" she asked.

"No, Precious. I have a different punishment in mind for you today."

"Will it hurt?"

"It won't be your favorite," he answered truthfully.

"I'm sorry," she told him. "I shouldn't have cheated."

"Daddy will punish you, and he'll forgive you."

She nodded sadly, giving him big puppy-dog eyes. Wraith steeled himself not to weaken. Her naughtiness had to be addressed.

"Come, lean on Daddy's chest," he instructed, turning her slightly until her spine rested against the front of him. "Now drape your knees over mine."

He helped her move into position with her legs spread across his. Wraith widened his thighs, splaying her legs farther apart. *Damn, I wish I had a mirror.* He pinpointed a place in front of the rocker to install one as he held her solidly in place when she tried to sit up. "Relax, Precious. Daddy's in charge, remember?"

"Daddy's in charge," she parroted and followed his instructions.

Wraith twisted the vibrator on. He ran it over Jam's belly before drawing a line down her abdomen. He rubbed it over her diaper-wrapped mound and heard her gasp in reaction as the hum diffused over her widely stretched pelvic tissues. Moving it lower, Wraith held it in place over her clitoral area.

"Daddy!" she whimpered.

"Not quite enough?" he asked, brushing it back and forth.

"No. Maybe if you took this off?" she asked, tugging at the cushioned garment she wore.

"Not going to happen, Caroline." As he stroked her with the vibrator, her wiggles intensified as she shifted in a vain attempt to strengthen the sensations.

"I don't like this, Daddy."

"That's what makes it a good punishment." Wraith lifted the vibrator and let her relax. She wouldn't like this at all. A few minutes later, he restarted it and repeated the process. This time, he pressed it a bit firmer on the decorations on the front.

"Not again, Daddy!" she protested.

"How many cards did I find in your panties?"

"Two."

"And how many total did you hide there?"

"Two," she promised him.

"Don't lie to Daddy. That would not be a smart move. Especially now." He kept his tone stern, concealing how adorable he thought his naughty Little was.

"Five. I had five," she confessed as her wiggles increased.

Wraith switched off the vibrator. He could tell when she recovered. Caroline relaxed. She turned her head to look back at him as she put the pieces of their conversation together.

"Five, Daddy. You're going to torture me five times?"

"Punish, Little girl."

"I'm really sorry," she told him.

"I know." Wraith turned the vibrator on for a third round.

By the last time, Caroline shook in his arms from need. Wraith whispered into her ear, "Are you going to cheat again?"

Her head thrashed back and forth as she held Jam to her face. Wraith slid a hand down the inside of her pull-up and tented it up from her skin. Using the tunnel he'd created, he moved the vibrator to press directly on her clit.

Her scream echoed in the quiet room as she convulsed into a

massive orgasm. Wraith removed the vibrator quickly as her body squirted into the padding from the force of her climax. Switching off the device, he set it on the table and pressed firmly on her bladder.

"No, Daddy," she cried as she lost control, flooding her diaper.

"Shush, Little girl. You're fine. Daddy's got you." Wraith stood and carried her to the changing table where he quickly cleaned her up and replaced her pull-up.

Returning to the rocker, he gave her a kiss before sliding the bottle's nipple into her mouth. "Suck, Caroline. You need some nourishment." He pulled her blanket free and draped it over her exposed skin.

With her hand tangled in the soft fabric, Caroline slowly lowered her eyelids as she drank her bottle. She had almost finished it when she fell asleep. Wraith continued to rock her for several minutes as he memorized the sight of his adult baby in his arms. Caroline was absolutely enchanting.

Rising, he tucked her into her crib and extinguished the lights. He'd let her nap until dinner. He'd schedule regular Little days for her. She'd responded perfectly.

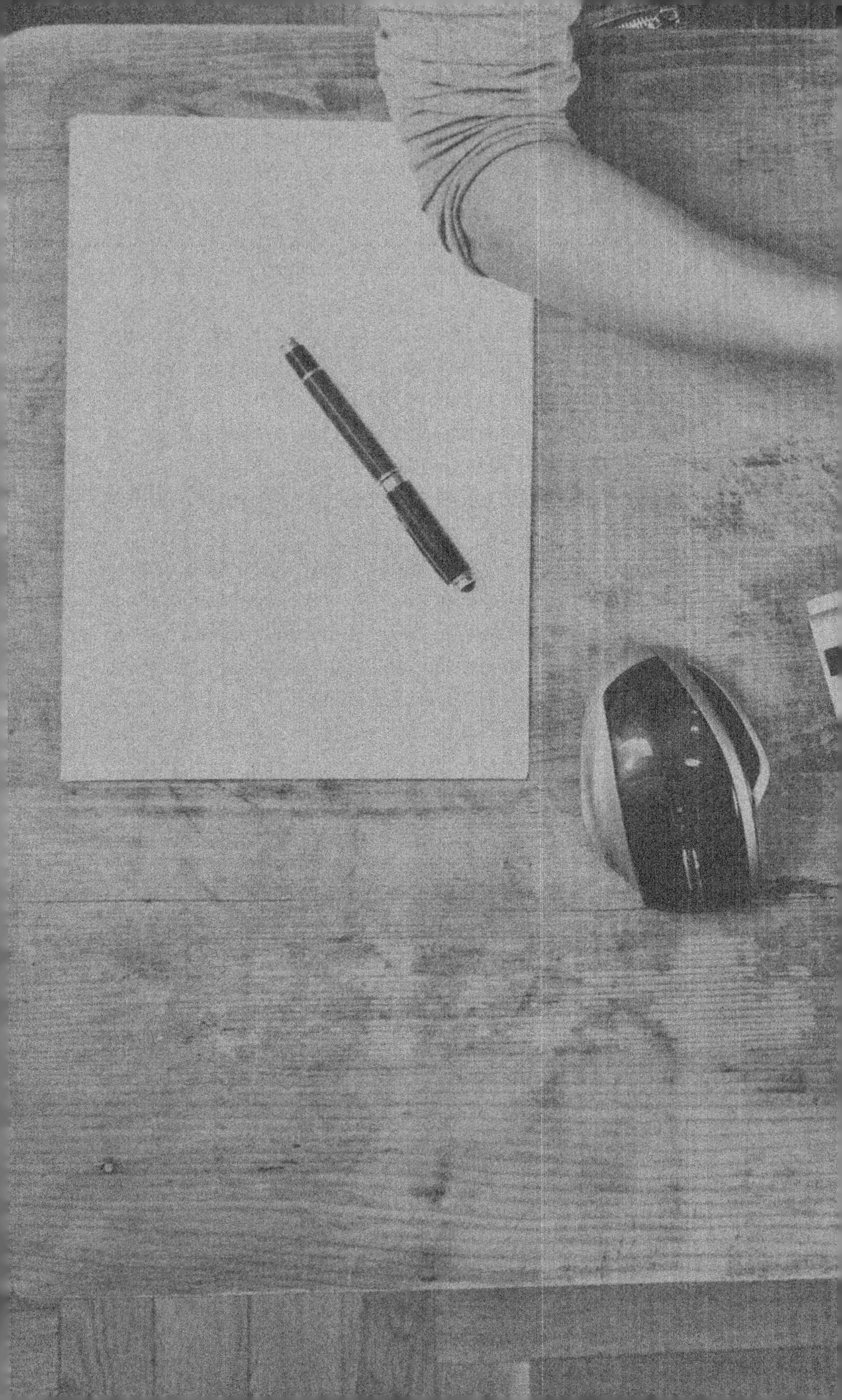

CHAPTER 18

This afternoon, Caroline had gotten horribly frustrated with the characters in her work in progress. The novel had lots of twists and turns she hadn't planned, but the hero and heroine kept getting into tough situations. By the time Wraith arrived home, she had given up and climbed on a stepladder to grab his bourbon.

"What are you doing, Little girl?" he asked from the kitchen doorway.

With the bottle in hand, Caroline spun around in surprise and wobbled in her position with a foot on the ladder and one on the countertop. Wraith rushed forward to catch her as she tumbled. "Whoopsie!" Caroline said with a giggle. "I saved the bottle."

"I'm glad we don't have shattered glass to deal with, Caroline, but I wouldn't want you in pieces."

"Probably not my favorite thing either, but a few more sips of this and I'd be okay," she anticipated.

"New rule. No climbing on ladders while Daddy's out," Wraith proclaimed and set her feet on the floor. He confiscated the bourbon and took a drink.

"Now. Why are we drinking?" he asked, raising an eyebrow

quizzically at her.

"No one will do what I tell them to do."

"I hate it when that happens. I usually knock a few heads together to put an end to that silliness. That stops the rebellion quickly."

"If only I could try that." Caroline grabbed the bottle back and swallowed again. "Bourbon helps."

"Until your head hurts in a few hours. I have a better suggestion for dealing with frustration."

"Really? What?"

"A bubble bath."

"How is that going to help?" she asked.

"There are magical properties in bubbles and warm water. I can prove it in fifteen minutes."

"You're not lying, are you?" she asked.

"Come on, Precious. We'll let the proof be in the pudding. Or in this case, in the bathwater."

A few minutes later, Wraith helped her undress as a cascade of water flooded into the tub. She loved his kisses and even the slap on her bottom to encourage her to settle into the fragrant water. Bubbles floated inches thick on the top. She had fun coaxing them into shapes and even blowing them across the tub.

"Hey, Little girl. I forgot to show you these." Wraith opened a small tub and dumped the contents into the water. Yellow duckies, a turtle, seashells, and even a mermaid floated on the surface of the water and hid in the foam.

"Daddy? Toys?"

Immediately, she started a search and rescue mission to round up everything. A flash of tan skin made her glance at the side. Her Daddy stood shirtless on the rug. He unfastened the button and zipper on his jeans.

"Are you going to take a bath with me?"

"Why not? Maybe I had a frustrating day too. I had characters not doing what I told them to."

She loved watching her Daddy get naked. His chiseled frame

was all hard shadows and bulging power. She'd never met anyone in that type of shape. Wiggling on the tub floor, she enjoyed her reaction to his attractiveness.

"You have to be the strongest man in the Devil Daddies MC. Make a muscle for me, Daddy."

Wraith winked and curled his fist up to show off his massive biceps. "There might be bigger arms in the Devils."

"Like mine?" Caroline flexed her arm and piled a mound of bubbles on top of it.

"That's impressive," Wraith said, stepping into the tub. "I'll sit over here so you don't beat me up."

"Aw, I wouldn't do that, Daddy. Just like you wouldn't punish me for climbing on the counter, right?"

"Oh, that deserves a spanking. But you're going to promise me you'll never do that again."

"Of course, Daddy. I'd never.... Wait, did you disappear to hide the stepladder?"

"You'll never find it," he promised.

"Daddy!"

"Come here, Precious. Bring your toys. Let's play and forget about the rest of the world, real and fictional."

In a flash, she sat next to him. "Here, Daddy. You can have this duck."

"Thanks, Little girl. You're so generous," he told her, eying the dozen floaties she kept for herself.

"I know. I'm an angel. That's the gang the Little girls should be in. The Devil's Angels. We could have leather cuts just like yours."

"That won't happen, Caroline."

"Why not?"

"No chance in hell," he elaborated.

"Wait until everyone finds their Littles. Then we Angels will band together and rise up!" Caroline thrust her fist out of the water, scattering suds in all directions.

"What if the Devil Daddy has a Little boy instead of a Little girl?" Wraith asked.

Slowly, Caroline's rigid protest arm deflated and plopped back into the bathtub. "He might not want to be called an Angel?"

"Maybe not."

"Fine. Those leather cuts are too heavy anyway. I'd be hunched over like an old lady in a year," she said, demonstrating. When she sat up, she had bubbles on the end of her nose. Caroline could barely see it if she concentrated.

"Let me help you before your eyes get stuck like that," Wraith said and wiped her nose clean.

"Thanks, Daddy. I don't think I could type like that. Oh! I've got it figured out. I have to get out now," she said, scrambling to return to her computer as a solution ricocheted into her brain, ending her roadblock.

Wraith grabbed her around the waist and held her in the tub before calling the assistant on his phone. "Hey, Siri. Open a Word document and write this down."

He had the best ideas. Caroline spoke quickly, outlining the simple solution she'd come up with to the assistant. Taking care of that before she could forget it helped her stop worrying.

"I'm done, Daddy."

"Siri, end recording."

Caroline leaned back on his chest, playing with the mermaid on her tummy. "I'm so much better now."

"I'm glad. By the way, how much bourbon did you drink?"

"I got trapped up there about fifteen minutes before you came home."

"Trapped?"

"Yeah. I couldn't figure out how to get to the floor without falling."

"So you kept drinking bourbon?" he asked, sounding incredulous.

"Hey, it's good bourbon." She snickered at his expression. "I'm teasing. I'd only had a couple of sips."

"That bourbon may have to disappear as well."

Her giggles filled the bathroom, and she turned to lever herself over Wraith, straddling his hips. She tickled him until he laughed along with her.

"Kiss me, Precious. Maybe you can convince me to put the bourbon on a lower shelf," Wraith suggested.

"Really?"

"Not ever going to happen," he confessed.

She gave him a few hundred kisses anyway. It turned out he was right. Bubbles did have a rejuvenating effect.

CHAPTER 19

On her way back to Wraith's side after a trip to the restroom at Inferno, Caroline waved at several people. She loved being a part of the group here. The bartenders were all amazing, and of course, the Devil Daddies kept an eye on her. Best of all, they were glad to see her too.

"Hey. Come dance," a male voice demanded.

That definitely wasn't Wraith's gravelly tone. Caroline glanced up in surprise. Now that the crowd was used to seeing her with Wraith, guys didn't approach her. Who'd want to mess with Wraith?

"Hey. Sorry. I'm with someone. I only boogie with him," Caroline answered politely and turned to walk away.

Caroline stared down at the firm hand squeezing her upper arm. "Ouch! Let me go. I said no."

"I wasn't inviting you. Consider it a demand." The man walked toward the dance floor, pulling Caroline after him.

She struggled to free herself, but he tightened his fingers. "Hey. Thank you for the compliment, but you really want to leave me alone."

"Right now, I want to dance with you."

He tugged her into his arms and swayed like they were

dancing to a romantic, slow song, even though the upbeat tempo of the music had others rocking around them at high speed. Caroline pushed hard.

"I said no!"

When the jerk laughed, Caroline looked around frantically. She made eye contact with Razor, who stood at the bar. *Please let him see the panic on my face.*

Immediately, Razor ran toward her, bellowing for Wraith. He elbowed a path through the dance floor.

"Back off, asshole!" Wraith shouted from behind her, drawing the man's attention.

Caroline knew the moment the jerk spotted the enormous man approaching. His eyes widened, and he immediately released his hold on her and backed up with his hands raised. She scurried away from the aggressive man so he couldn't grab her again. She couldn't get to Wraith as he approached from the opposite direction. Several of the dancers put themselves between her and her assailant. While she appreciated the buffer, she had to see what happened.

The music stopped, and the DJ announced, "This won't be pretty." Everyone turned to the dance floor as a hush fell over the crowd.

"I'm not hurt," Caroline yelled to Wraith as she struggled to meet his gaze through the crowd.

"You made one hell of a mistake," Wraith told the jerk. Members from the Devil Daddies MC surrounded her assailant and swept him outside.

A pathway opened between Caroline and Wraith. She ran forward to jump into his arms. His expression scared her. Raw violence shone from his gaze.

"I'm okay, Wraith. Just make him leave."

Wraith took a moment to run his hands over her. Caroline tried not to wince as he touched the rising welts on her arms. "He's going to pay for hurting you."

Focusing over her shoulder, Wraith asked, "Watch her for me?"

Razor nodded before answering. "You got it."

"Stay with Razor."

"Wraith, please. Don't hurt him. I'm okay."

"No one touches my Little girl," Wraith told her softly. "He'll learn."

"They've got him in the far-right parking lot."

Jerking to look to the side, Caroline spotted Lucien. He'd come down from his office on the second floor. This wasn't good.

"Lucien, talk some sense into him," she pleaded.

"That won't happen," Lucien informed her in a flat tone that didn't allow her to argue. He signaled the DJ to restart the music.

"Come on, Caroline. Let me make sure you're okay." Razor escorted her off the dance floor as everyone resumed dancing, almost as if nothing had happened.

"I don't want Wraith to get in trouble," Caroline told Razor as he led her into a small office near the kitchen and grabbed a large first aid kit from the wall.

"He'll be fine. Let's worry about you," Razor said firmly. He ran his hands over her arms. "You'll have some bruises here. That's going to piss Wraith off until they heal."

"I'm fine," Caroline said, eager to go find Wraith.

"He's going to come collect you here when he's finished. Let's put some ice on these bruises. Need a painkiller?"

"My head hurts," she admitted.

"Did he hit you?" Razor asked, bristling. He cupped her chin and checked out her eyes.

"No. I think it's the tension."

"I'm sorry, Caroline. Let's get some medicine in you." He grabbed a bottle of water from the fridge and handed her two tablets. After watching her take them, he left the office to grab some ice. Razor was back before she could formulate a plan to go intercede in whatever was going on in the parking lot.

"Stop fretting about it. Wraith will take care of him. Tell me about yourself, Caroline. We haven't had time to talk."

He was distracting her.

"How about if you tell me about you? You're a real doctor?" Caroline had put that together from what she'd overheard at Inferno.

"I am." He wrapped an ice pack around her upper arm with colorful sports wrap before moving on to the other.

"What kind?"

"I'm an MD and a PhD."

"You really liked college."

"I did."

"What's your PhD in?" she asked, completely intrigued.

"Psychology."

"And you're a Daddy?" When he gave her a sharp look, she backpedaled. "You don't have to answer me, of course. You are part of the Devil *Daddies* MC," she pointed out.

"I am." Razor finished her right arm and leaned back in the office chair he'd snagged from behind the desk.

His gaze seemed to see through her. Did that go hand in hand with being a shrink? She suspected little got past him.

"So, I'm not crazy for being a Little?" she asked.

"Are you happy?"

"More so than I've ever been," she answered, smiling for the first time since she'd run into that jerk in the hall.

"Then you're what you're supposed to be," he assured her.

"Feeling better?"

"Yes. Thank you. Do I sit here and wait for Wraith?"

"He'll come get you in a few minutes. Mind if I stay with you? You never told me about you."

"I'm a writer. Romance novels," she said, waiting for the inevitable comment about trashy books.

"I bet that's challenging and fun at the same time. What's your process?" Razor asked, seeming truly interested.

Right there, Caroline decided she liked Razor. He didn't

think she was crazy, and he didn't make snap judgements about her because she wrote spicy stories. She opened her mouth to answer his question.

"She'll educate you on publishing later, Razor. I'm going to take my girl to our cabin."

"Wraith!" Caroline had jumped to her feet at the sound of his voice. She rushed forward to throw her arms around his waist and hug him tight.

"Hi, Precious. You still doing alright? Razor?" Wraith checked with his MC brother as if he suspected she might not tell him the truth.

"She'll have some bruises, but she'll live to write another sex scene," Razor informed him. "Caroline should rest tonight. That was frightening for her."

"Thanks, Razor. Ready to go home, Caroline?"

"Yes." She touched her fingers to a few red spots on his face. She'd kiss them better when they were alone.

Wraith had obviously physically attacked the man. While she hated the thought of him getting in trouble for hurting someone, Caroline had to admit to herself that it was hot that he'd stood up for her. No one had ever put themselves in harm's way for her.

"I think you need to take it easy tonight too. Should we have Razor strap ice packs on you?"

"No need." Wraith refused, stepping back to take her hand. "Are you okay to hold on to me?"

"Yes. My arms are a bit bruised. He scared me more than injured me."

"Asshole. Who thinks a woman's going to respond well to a caveman approach? Let's go home, Little girl."

Wraith held out his hand to Razor. "Thanks, brother. I owe you one."

"I'll collect when I find my Little," the quiet man answered with a single downward nod.

"They don't need you at the door?" she asked.

"No, Precious. They'll be fine without me. You will always be more important to me than anything else."

"Even the Devil Daddies?"

"Shhh! Don't tell them. They'll get all butt hurt," he teased as he nodded.

Caroline pretended to zip her lips closed.

"Good girl."

How did his praise make everything else disappear? She clung to him as they walked out the door.

"Caroline! Finally!"

Crap! She knew that voice. Adam stood outside the front entrance. Wraith automatically pulled her behind him. "Wait, Wraith. It's okay."

Maneuvering around his bulk, Caroline met Adam's gaze directly. How could she have been so dumb to marry this guy? "What do you want, Adam?"

"I need money, Caroline."

"I give you a percentage of the revenue from the books I wrote while we were married. You divorced me, remember? You don't get anything else."

"Come on, honey."

Wraith growled and shifted closer.

Adam retreated a foot. "Control your goon, Caroline."

Caroline put out an arm to block Wraith from showing him how a goon would take care of him. "You really don't want to call him names, Adam. Go away. I got a message from my lawyer yesterday that the judge had refused to hear your request for additional money. I'm sure your attorney received the same notification. It's over. Move on. If you don't, I'll pull the books you get a percentage off the market."

"You'd lose those earnings," Adam said. His face revealed his shock at that idea.

"And so would you. As a bonus, I'd never have to deal with you. So, make your decision. Get some money or be a jerk and end up with *nothing*." Caroline stressed that last word. She was done putting up with his garbage.

"Caroline, honey...."

"Call her that one more time and I'm going to remove your teeth," Wraith promised grimly.

Adam stared at Caroline, obviously wondering whether she would allow that to happen. Her expression must have answered the question. "Okay. I'll back off. I won't contact you, but you have to help me. I got involved in a scam, and now they're after me."

"You're going to have to figure this out yourself, Adam. If I bail you out now, you'll return over and over. We're not married any more. By *your* choice. Stop making crappy decisions."

"You've changed, Caroline. Hanging out with these bikers isn't good for you," Adam told her.

"Better than strippers and scammers," Wraith said with a glower.

"Caroline, after all I did for you...." Adam appealed to her good nature.

"You are an idiot, Adam. You did nothing for me. If you have anything else to say to me, contact my lawyer. Don't come to Inferno. I won't ask Wraith to stand down again," Caroline warned.

"Ditto."

How could one word carry so much menace? Caroline turned to see Lucien standing to the side with a posse of Devil Daddies behind him. The biker appeared lethal. Caroline shivered and pressed herself to Wraith as he wrapped his arm around her.

To his credit, Adam didn't run. He turned and walked briskly down the paved walkway toward the parking lot. Caroline was pleased to see him disappear into the rows of cars without ever looking back. Maybe he'd gotten the message.

CHAPTER 20

Driving into the garage, Caroline spotted Wraith's bike. He was home early. A thrill that never faded at the prospect of spending time with her Daddy flooded into her. He was her everything. Her lover, cheerleader, best friend, and Daddy. *Most spectacular one-night stand in history.*

She spotted a piece of paper taped to the interior door leading to the kitchen. Was that a lollipop? Automatically, Caroline tried to read it as she pulled her car inside. When she couldn't see the writing clearly, she grabbed her purse and thrust the vehicle door open. She darted toward the entrance and read:

Choose your adventure…

Daddy's going to make you come until the romance novel heroes you create look like total novices. Will you choose the kitchen table? You'll make a tasty snack. Or would you prefer to be bound to Daddy's bed where he has total control? Take the lollipop. Suck it while you decide. Knock once for table. Two for silken rope.

. . .

Caroline followed his directions without questioning them. She removed the sucker from the paper and unwrapped it. *Mmm! Apple.* Her favorite flavor. Caroline reread the note and realized Wraith had to be on the other side of the door, waiting to hear her answer. Silently, she pressed her hand against the wood.

So, the kitchen table or being bound to Wraith's bed? The kitchen held all sorts of implements Wraith enjoyed using to tease and punish her. The thin wooden spoon was so stingy. Caroline squeezed her legs together as her slick juices welled in response to that arousing memory. Sitting at the table for a meal after he'd done filthy things to her always made her blush for days.

She'd asked him about the rings in the headboard last night. Wraith had winked at her and reminded her that he enjoyed restraining her on her changing table. Caroline always liked it too.

Sucking furiously on her lollipop, she made her decision. Knock! Knock!

Did she have to wait? Caroline hesitated for a moment before opening the door. A trail of rose petals led into the cabin. She inhaled, absorbing the beautiful fragrance as she passed the kitchen table decorated with a heart-shaped scattering of the red petals.

Caroline dropped the apple sucker in the trash to concentrate on the floral scent. She licked her lips, anticipating the kisses her Daddy would share with her. It still surprised her that the immense biker had chosen her. She hadn't told him yet, but she loved Wraith with such intensity her heart hurt sometimes just watching him.

She peeked around the corner and saw him propped up on pink satiny pillows. "You got me pillows."

"I did. You chose to be brave. Come here, Precious. Let me unwrap my present."

Walking forward to him, Caroline studied his face. Wraith was a complicated man. She didn't believe she'd ever discover everything about him. Surprisingly, that didn't bother her. It turned her on.

"Turn that brain off, Little girl. You're thinking too hard."

Nodding, she stopped in front of him. He undressed her slowly, lavishing kisses on her skin as he revealed it. Caroline closed her eyes to savor his caresses. His hands on her body with the rasp of his callouses sent shivery sensations through her. He worshiped her, not seeing any of the numerous flaws that stood out to her in the mirror.

"Look at me, Caroline," he ordered in that gravelly voice she loved.

"Yes, Daddy."

"Crawl on the bed, Precious. Kneel facing the pillows."

"Aren't you going to undress?" she asked, glancing over her shoulder as she followed his directions.

"Yes. First, I'm going to punish you."

Freezing, she protested, "I've been good."

"Good girls get spankings too."

"I thought you were going to tie me up..." Her voice trailed off as he unfastened his belt and tugged it free. Caroline swallowed hard as he dropped the belt next to her on the bed. They'd never played with a belt before. Nervous, she shifted back and forth. Was he going to use it now?

"That's next."

He opened the nightstand drawer and pulled out a pink cord. Brushing it over her skin, he showed her how it would feel as if sensing she needed that. An unfamiliar thrill ran through her. She bit her lip to hold back a moan.

"Give me your wrists, Caroline."

He threaded the rope through the center ring in the headboard. When he held out a powerful hand for hers, Caroline's emotions ricocheted in all directions. Excitement. Fear of the unknown. Arousal. Wraith wound the cord carefully around her lower arms, reassuring her that he would always keep her safe.

She couldn't wait to experience what he had planned. Caroline shifted restlessly. Sex with Wraith was hotter than any scene she could create. The jerk of him cinching the knot made her gaze dart from the pink rope to his face.

"Daddy will let you go whenever you need him to. All play stops when you say your safeword. Do you remember it, Precious?"

"Fire."

"Good girl. Shift forward. I want you on your hands and knees. Move your thighs apart. More. Perfect. Now, drop down to your forearms." His hands stroked over her to smooth over the curve of her full bottom. "The first time we met, I noticed this delectable ass. Now, it's mine."

Channeling her sassy side, she wiggled her butt under his touch.

"I can't wait to see how you react to my belt, Little girl. This butt will look amazing with red stripes," he told her as he tightened the cord. Wraith placed one knee on the bed to get closer. He wrapped a powerful arm around her and supported her as he drew her hands forward until she stretched toward the headboard. Gently, he lowered her chest to the comforter.

"Tug on the rope, Precious. See if you can get away."

As his hands caressed her spine, Caroline pulled against the binding. She shook her head to tell him she was secure. She was on her knees with her breasts pressed to the mattress and her hands tied in front of her, and the vulnerability of her position struck her as he walked around the bed. She heard him pause behind her and knew Wraith had a clear view of her pussy and bottom.

The rasp of his zipper and a deep groan made her glance back at him. Wraith stood with his hand gripping his thick shaft. He dragged a rough hand from base to tip. Her embarrassment evaporated. He was so into her. She absolutely loved how he looked at her.

"Daddy, please."

That spurred him to move. Throwing his clothes around the

room, Wraith moved to her side. His bulk seemed larger uncontained by fabric. He grabbed the belt in one powerful hand and shook it out.

With anyone else, Caroline would have been petrified. With Wraith, her arousal level skyrocketed through the roof. She jumped when he snapped the leather strip. The sound reverberated through the quiet space.

He didn't warn her. The next sound came from the belt striking her bottom. Instant fire erupted on her skin. Gasping, she tried to process the sensation. A second impact made her bolt forward.

Wraith's arm wrapped under her stomach, holding her in place. She heard a dull thud, and his other hand stroked over her punished skin. His palm both smoothed and ignited the fiery tingles. He'd dropped the belt.

"You're gorgeous with marks, Little girl."

Without any preliminaries, he placed his cock at her entrance and plunged into her. Grabbing a handful of hair, Wraith pulled her back, impaling her deeper than ever before. The sting of her scalp blended with the sizzle of him brushing against her strapped skin, drawing a moan from her lips.

"Daddy," she whispered as her finger wrapped around the rope binding her.

"You can take everything, Precious. You deserve it all," he praised her before withdrawing to her entrance. He hesitated there. The desire to come consumed her.

"Fuck me, Daddy. I need you."

He thrust forward and set a fast pace. One hand held her so securely she suspected he'd leave bruises on her hip. The other tugged her hair, rocking her to meet his thrusts.

The tingles that preceded her orgasm began to gather. Caroline closed her eyes to focus. Wraith ground his thick root against her clit. When he released her side to swat her bottom, pleasure exploded over her as her tight channel clamped down on his cock.

"Fuck, Little girl. So good."

He held her secure as she shook with the force of her climax. When she could think, Caroline protested as Wraith withdrew from her. "Nooo."

"Hold on, Precious. I need to see your face."

Wraith helped her slide off her knees and roll to stretch out on her back. He crawled over her and kissed her hard. "Are your arms okay?"

She nodded before urging, "More, Daddy."

His slow grin made her daring. She wiggled her shoulders to jostle her breasts.

"Temptress."

Settling himself between her legs, Wraith entered her slowly, making her feel every inch of his length. Caroline wrapped her legs around his waist and met each thrust. His moves rebuilt the excitement inside her. She missed touching him but loved his dominance.

Loved him.

Caroline wanted to tell him. She met his heated gaze. "Daddy, I love you."

"Damn it, Caroline. I need to have your hands on me."

His words could have meant something bad, but the tender expression in his eyes revealed everything to her. She nodded. "Please, Daddy."

Wraith withdrew and quickly untied her wrists and kissed her palms before setting them down on his shoulders. "Say it again, Little girl."

"I love you, Daddy."

"Fucking hell. I didn't think you'd ever say it. I'm going to make you tell me that every freaking day! I realized I loved you in the middle of the bourbon incident," he told her before kissing her with such heat to show her how much he cared about her. He settled back between her thighs and filled her once again.

The edgy thrill of bondage flipped on its head as he made love to her as if she were the most precious thing in his life.

Caroline caressed him, returning the pleasure he lavished on her. When the sensations overwhelmed her, Wraith tenderly wiped the tears away from her cheeks as their bodies shuddered against each other.

"Such a good girl. I love you, Caroline."

"I love you so much, Daddy."

"You're going to love me even more when you see the nursery decorations above your changing table."

"What? I didn't notice anything," she wiggled toward the edge of the bed.

"Daddy will carry you in there in a few minutes to get you all cleaned up to go to sleep," he promised, towing her back to recover by his side.

When he'd caught her getting up after their lovemaking to use the toilet and wash off her intimate spaces, Wraith had taken over to make her more comfortable. Now, he waited until she was almost asleep to scoop her up in his powerful arms to place her first on the potty and then on her changing table. As he gently stretched her on the padded top, he clicked on the glowing nightlight and pointed to the decorations.

"Can you spot something new on the wall?" he asked as he grabbed a wipe from the warmer.

"Snails!" She reached forward to run her fingers lightly across the brightly colored, cartoon snails that now crawled over the paint. "Thank you. I love them."

"Anything to make my Little girl happy." Wraith kissed her tummy before singing softly to her. The soft tune in his deep voice was magical in its effectiveness to lull her back to sleep. Caroline could barely keep her eyes open as he tucked her back in bed. How had she ever slept without him?

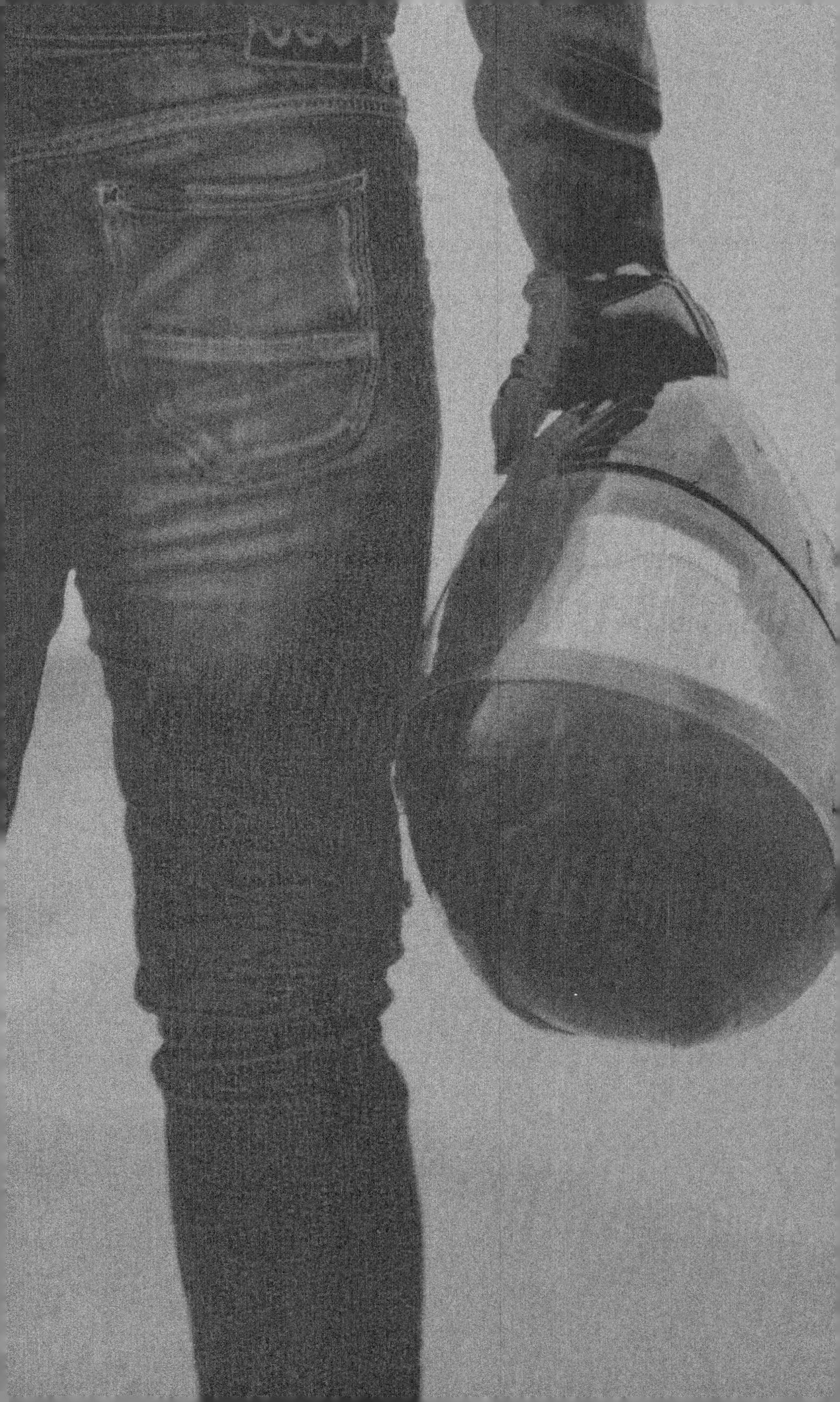

EPILOGUE

Wraith watched Caroline shine with pride and glowered at the men who attempted to get her attention. He was sitting right here. Wraith wasn't used to people missing his presence. Thank goodness they backed down quickly when he sent a targeted glance their direction. Lucien would take him off the door if he bashed too many skulls together.

"Everyone's looking at me differently, Daddy," Caroline hissed when there was a break in the customers arriving.

"You're sparkling, Little girl. I'll take credit for that," Wraith told her with a wink.

"I'm trying to appear normal."

"Precious, you couldn't be normal if you tried. You're a bad-biker-loving romance author. Those are always the wild ones."

"Wraith!" she protested before admitting, "I do love my Devil Daddy."

He rewarded her with a hard kiss. A woman had a crack at skirting past him while he was distracted. Wraith put out a powerful arm to block her path and finished kissing his Little girl.

Scythe appeared to screen the guests. "ID."

When Wraith turned back to the woman, Caroline gripped his thigh enticingly. He sent a stern message to his cock to wait until later before addressing the customer, "Not cool."

Scythe scanned the ID she had given him. Without a word, Scythe handed it to Wraith. It did not reflect the current image of the heavily made-up woman, wearing a strappy dress that revealed hints of silky skin. He recognized the person in the picture. He'd turned away the woman who wore knee-length, full skirts with an old-fashioned cardigan a couple of times at least. Those uptight clients didn't fit in well with the usual Inferno clientele and usually created problems.

He met the woman's gaze and read hopelessness in her eyes. Another strike against her. Desperation and alcohol didn't mix successfully. He opened his mouth to refuse her, but Caroline's fingers dug into his thigh. When he met her gaze, his Little girl nodded.

Magnanimously, Wraith handed her ID back and said, "Welcome to Inferno. Don't cause trouble."

"No, sir. Thank you." The woman disappeared quickly into the crowd.

"What the fuck, Wraith?" Scythe asked.

"She needed to be here," Caroline said quickly.

Wraith waved his hand Caroline's way, endorsing her statement.

Scythe stalked off, shaking his head. Wraith would keep an eye on her. Was he wrong or did Scythe react strongly to the woman? Caroline jumped off her stool and boogied to the music as her favorite song came on, erasing any concern from Wraith's mind.

Scythe would handle her.

Thank you for reading Wraith: Devil Daddies MC 1!

Don't miss future sweet and steamy Daddy stories by Pepper North? Subscribe to my newsletter!

Get ready for the next story in the Devil Daddies MC series: Scythe: Devil Daddies MC 2!

If you want something moved, you'll have to check with Scythe.

Scythe comes from old-fashioned country life. His word is his bond, and he challenges any wrong he encounters. Lying to Scythe is not a good idea. When he spots a heavily made-up woman wearing an obvious disguise, he knows something's up. Why is she pretending to be someone she isn't?

Winnie Bradley can't believe she made it into Inferno after being turned away by the bouncer twice for being too churchy. So what if her clothes don't flash all her body parts? Or any of them. Tonight's borrowed outfit is too drafty to be comfortable. She just needs to broker a deal for her stepdad's collection before her nerve evaporates. If only that hot biker wouldn't scowl at her!

The members of the Devil Daddies MC will risk all to secure two things: special acquisitions and women with a Little side.

Preorder yours NOW!

Read more from Pepper North

Fated Dragon Daddies

Change is coming to Wyvern.
A centuries-old pact between the founders and their powerful allies could save the inhabitants of the city once again, but only a dragon Daddy can truly guard his mate from harm.

Shadowridge Guardians

Combining the sizzling talents of bestselling authors Pepper North, Kate Oliver, and Becca Jameson, the Shadowridge Guardians are guaranteed to give you a thrill and leave you dreaming of your own throbbing motorcycle joyride.

Are you daring enough to ride with a club of rough, growly, commanding men? The protective Daddies of the Shadowridge Guardians Motorcycle Club will stop at nothing to ensure the safety and protection of everything that belongs to them: their Littles, their club, and their town. Throw in some sassy, naughty, mischievous women who won't hesitate to serve their fair share of attitude even in the face of looming danger, and this brand new MC Romance series is ready to ignite!

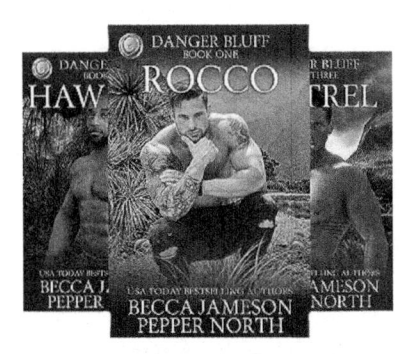

Danger Bluff

Welcome to Danger Bluff where a mysterious billionaire brings together a hand-selected team of men at an abandoned resort in New Zealand. They each owe him a marker. And they all have something in common—a dominant shared code to nurture and protect. They will repay their debts one by one, finding love along the way.

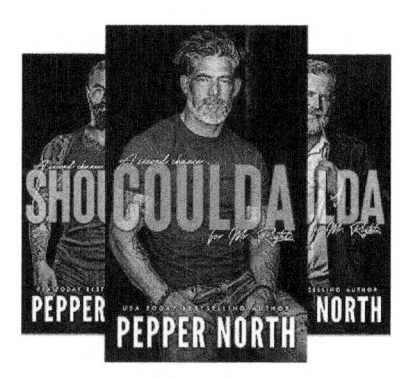

A Second Chance For Mr. Right

For some, there is a second chance at having Mr. Right. Coulda, Shoulda, Woulda explores a world of connections that can't exist... until they do. Forbidden love abounds when these Daddy Doms refuse to live with regret and claim the women who own their hearts.

Little Cakes

Welcome to Little Cakes, the bakery that plays Daddy matchmaker! Little Cakes is a sweet and satisfying series, but dare to taste only if you like delicious Daddies, luscious Littles, and guaranteed happily-ever-afters.

Dr. Richards' Littles®

A beloved age play series that features Littles who find their forever Daddies and Mommies. Dr. Richards guides and supports their efforts to keep their Littles happy and healthy.

Note: Zoey; Dr. Richards' Littles® 1 is available FREE on Pepper's website:
4PepperNorth.club

Dr. Richards' Littles®
is a registered trademark of
With A Wink Publishing, LLC.
All rights reserved.

SANCTUM

Pepper North introduces you to an age play community that is isolated from the surrounding world. Here Littles can be Little, and Daddies can care for their Littles and keep them protected from the outside world.

Soldier Daddies

What private mission are these elite soldiers undertaking? They're all searching for their perfect Little girl.

The Keepers

This series from Pepper North is a twist on contemporary age play romances. Here are the stories of humans cared for by specially selected Keepers of an alien race. These are science fiction novels that age play readers will love!

The Magic of Twelve

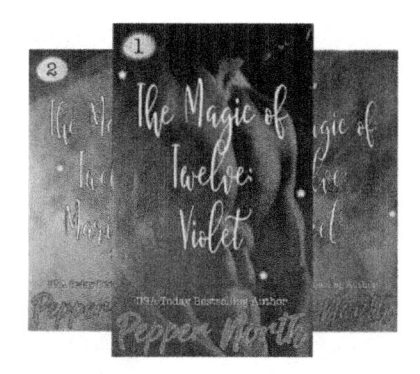

The Magic of Twelve features the stories of twelve women transported on their 22nd birthday to a new life as the droblin (cherished Little one) of a Sorcerer of Bairn. These magic wielders have waited a long time to take complete care of their droblin's needs. They will protect their precious one to their last drop of magic from a growing menace. Each novel is a complete story.

Ever just gone for it? That's what *USA Today* Bestselling Author Pepper North did in 2017 when she posted a book for sale on Amazon without telling anyone. Thanks to her amazing fans, the support of the writing community, Mr. North, and a killer schedule, she has now written more than 180 books!
Enjoy contemporary, paranormal, dark, and erotic romances that are both sweet and steamy? Pepper will convert you into one of her loyal readers. What's coming in the future? A Daddypalooza!

Sign up for Pepper North's newsletter

Like Pepper North on Facebook

Join Pepper's Readers' Group for insider information and giveaways!

Follow Pepper everywhere!

Amazon Author Page
BookBub
FaceBook
GoodReads
Instagram
TikToc
Twitter
YouTube
Visit Pepper's website for a current checklist of books!

Printed in Great Britain
by Amazon